SENIOR DROPOUT

SENIOR DROPOUT

by
JAMES L. SUMMERS

THE WESTMINSTER PRESS
Philadelphia

LIBRARY OF CONGRESS CATALOG CARD No. 65-16495

PUBLISHED BY THE WESTMINSTER PRESS ®
PHILADELPHIA, PENNSYLVANIA

PRINTED IN THE UNITED STATES OF AMERICA

FOR MARY PFEIFFER

SENIOR DROPOUT

1

NEBRASKA WAS an alien land by night, with the dark towns all alike in the flat prairie. They huddled in monotonous solitude on one side of the highway across from the railroad tracks. Lon Renton had slept for a time, lulled by the stale air, the sprawled and sleeping people, and the ceaseless drone and thrust as the huge bus rammed down the tunnel of its own headlights.

He had been awake for hours, sitting without movement to stare out of the grimy window at nothing. He was exhausted and he felt dirty, although he had changed in the rest room at the last stop. Where had that been? Wyoming? It didn't matter—or at least that was what Lon thought.

Beside him, Mr. Haley snored softly, sprawled out all over the reclined seat and into Lon's space. His odor seeped out pervasively with that definite suggestion of old vegetable soup, with beef, more pungent than all the other vagrant smells of a transcontinental bus.

Mr. Haley had joined the party at Laramie, with the announced intention of visiting his sister in Chicago. His face was as narrow and hard as a flint hatchet, a solid American from the last frontier—as he let everyone know at once. He believed in all that had been done in years gone by, and in nothing that was being done today. He declared his faith aloud with the zest of men shooting redskins for sport.

A sleepy sailor had told him flatly, "Mac, why don't you button your mouth and let me alone!"

Mr. Haley had done that, grumbling about how the services had deteriorated since he was a kid in the War, which was World War I, as Lon discovered endlessly thereafter. Young Joe Haley had wiped out more than one machine-gun nest manned by the ferocious Boche, and he didn't intend to let a seatmate forget it. That had taken real guts—something the soft youth of today didn't possess as they roamed America's streets and made them unsafe.

Although Haley's snores were annoying, Lon was glad that the old man slept. It gave him time to think—about Thelma and his father waiting for him in Milwaukee, about Greyrock behind him in California, about everything. All the points of arrival and departure in his life were here in the bus with him, none of them clear. There wasn't any meaning in what had happened or what was likely to happen soon—not to Lon Renton.

He shrugged elaborately, perhaps to gain more seat comfort but more likely to reinforce his complete diffidence. He was used to playing it cool toward everyone so nobody could know what he was thinking or ever catch him in an emotional relapse toward childhood. Lon was seventeen and already life had taught him to bear that age upward toward the world and to hide whatever real

10

feeling he had and turn it inside out before he even knew what it was himself. Nobody, but nobody at all, was ever going to catch Lon Renton with the vulnerable truth showing again.

He saw that a gray dawn was up across the land and that they were no longer spinning across country so flat that it was like being below the rim of an enormous plate. Hills had been born, first gently rolling and then lifting more into the percentages, so that the driver needed to hit the gears. Around him people aware of the change had begun to awaken, but Mr. Haley snored on.

The sickly morning light reminded Lon of that day in Greyrock when his dad's letter had come with the part Thelma had written below in her perfect hand. His only reaction to their plan was to feel that the future had taken the flip side of the same record, and would run down a new groove of their version of the same tune.

Involuntarily, Lon shook his head. He was hard as glass, he guessed, in the way that politicians and newspapers claimed all young people were these days. But what the surveys never admitted was that kids needed every link of the protective armor they wore, the harder the better. If a guy let them see what he really was inside, or if he trusted them enough to ask for help, he was done right there.

It would be like that one time when he had told the truth at Greyrock right after his father had left him alone in the room in Pershing Hall.

"Take care of yourself, Lonny." That was all Harold Renton had said.

Then his dad had gone back to the car and set out on his crazy trip across the country, revisiting scenes of his own youth and in all that time writing only three letters, none of which made sense to a son.

From the casemented window, Lon had watched his father go. After the car killed a right around the corner of the administration building, it disappeared toward the front gate. He had sat down hard on the narrow bed. The hurting, iron tears had begun slowly until they had become mixed with that terrible summer at the beach, and then nothing could stop them.

That was how Captain Keith Dart had found Lon because he'd walked in without rapping at the door—the accepted Greyrock technique, as a person discovered soon enough. Dart was the counselor for Pershing Hall and drill officer for the whole stupid cadet corps. If the door had been locked, he would have used his passkey.

"What's the trouble, Renton?" the captain had demanded, and that was the first Lon knew of his presence.

He glanced up with shock and surprise and tried to pull himself into a semblance of order. "Nothing," he'd said, horribly aware of how his breath jerked and trembled, but making a real try.

"Nothing, *sir*," Captain Dart corrected. "That's what you mean, isn't it?"

Lon had gotten his first good look at the captain then, and in two years at Greyrock the image never changed. The glitter of his polished boots matched his small glassy eyes. His cheeks were pink as baby skin, although he was tanned deeply everywhere else, with dark brown hair bristling into splashed gray. Mainly, though, Lon noticed his mouth, which was too small to be real, with small perfect teeth to match.

12

"Yes," he'd said, "that's what I mean."

"Yes, *sir*," Captain Dart corrected again, softening his tone until the "s" sound whistled. "Here at Greyrock, Renton, we observe military courtesy to all superior officers."

"Yes—" Lon said, pausing into a silence that allowed his cheap wristwatch to tick into the room on its frantic balance wheel. It had sounded like a desperate little animal, Lon still remembered here on this bus. "—sir," he had finished.

Somewhere in modern life a young guy learned sooner or later to distrust any emotion, and the Captain Darts helped him. Lonely self-pity could turn to a silent, smouldering rage that burned inside a person like those coal mine fires burned for years in the deep heart of a mountain.

Captain Dart's unit of the National Guard had been federalized during World War II, and the uniform he wore was of his own choice but close to the real thing. The cadets wore Greyrock blue, naturally, piped and slashed with red and desecrated with a double row of brass buttons down the front until a kid looked like a trained monkey who has lost his tin cup. But Dart's outfit was tailor-made of Pacific tan, with riding boots and a chauffeur's cap decorated with gold braid. Lon learned soon enough that he also usually carried a swagger stick out on the drill field, and the drums and brass horns in his blood were enough to turn a strong stomach sick.

"Sit down, Cadet Renton," he'd snapped now. "As you were."

"As I was?" Lon had asked foolishly. "How—how was I?" adding "sir?"

Probably his jaw had fallen open because Captain Dart grinned in genuine amusement, with both corners of that awful mouth turned up into an incredible half circle. It was an expression every pitiful stupe at Greyrock knew better than his own face; he got to know it for canting an ancient Springfield rifle a little out of line—for getting dirt on the ridiculous white gloves—for smiling himself. He learned its line and consequences for doing anything at all that was human and decent and natural.

"You were sitting on the bed, Cadet Renton, against regulations, and blubbering like a fat baby," Captain Dart explained by syllables. "A lot of our new boys do that on the first day—the younger ones, Renton, the Second Platoon men; it's not uncommon at all."

He stopped, looking expectant, so Lon said nothing.

Then, "As you were, Cadet Renton," Captain Dart shot out suddenly. "Sit!"

The sky had lightened and the hills of eastern Nebraska were waves in a strange sea, but Lon was far away from there, reliving his own sick shame that day and every day while Greyrock taught him. Discipline, they'd called it! Respect for authority!

He had sat down facing Captain Dart, with the word "sir" ready at his lips like something indescribably dirty. He had watched the man take the narrow desk chair, turn it around and straddle the back, facing him. He heard that voice—the coddling, shocking, nauseating tone of a phony adult.

"I had a nice talk with your father, Renton," said the captain. "Your mother died this summer, didn't she?"

Lon had looked up with widening eyes, his gasp choking out in unrestrained pain. Those words didn't belong in

14

Dart's mouth or in this terrible room. Nobody at Greyrock knew his mother. He had a wrenching sense of loss, as if his only precious possession had been stolen from him by force.

"Isn't that so, Cadet Renton?" the captain repeated softly. "Your mother was operated on for cancer and she died in the Mercy Hospital in Los Angeles."

Suddenly for Lon the beach was there with its slow green rollers spuming into white surf. He and his brother, Frank, had gone down there again while they were waiting for news. Frank was just out of college—business administration—and had been able to come home, but Marlene and Bob had their own families to worry about and stayed up north.

The beach at Clifton was rocky and nearly deserted most of the time, and Frank was a natural show-off. He always had to prove himself to everyone, especially a young brother. They would swim a while together, but then Frank had to take off by himself and go outward beyond the breakers—a mile—two miles—while Lon stood alone on the beach and strained his eyes into the westward sun, trying to place that bobbing head and shoulders lost in the swells. Lost—lost—

Fear! That was the poison a person had hidden within his skin—right up to a guy's throat! That was the weakness he kept from their sight if he could: he never let them know how scared he was!

And when Frank would come back, walking out of the surf with the spume disappearing through the soft, black, curling hairs on his wide chest, he would grin in a reckless way at a brother six years younger, the smile confident and wide across strong teeth. Then he had to remember

15

too, and say, "We'd better go back to the house and find out how Mom is today, kid. Too bad you didn't swim out there with me. It's great beyond the breakers."

Finally the day had come when his father came back from the hospital and sank heavily into a chair. Lon could still hear his voice and always would, sounding old and beaten at last.

"Your mother?" strangely; far away. "Your mother is dead!"

At Greyrock, Lon couldn't answer Dart; at least he hadn't been that much a coward. Instead he'd sat there stunned and cold as ice, feeling as if he were going to vomit right at the captain's feet and remembering the note his mother had written to each one of them.

His had said, "Be a good boy and brush your teeth every day." That was all, and it was burned into his mind forever as he searched and searched it for a meaning beyond those childish words. There had to be something more than that between his mother and him to match the pain and the yearning. It wasn't for a guy just turned fifteen, standing six feet tall; it was for a little kid with building blocks and a red wagon. His own mother had to know him better than that, didn't she? Didn't she?

On a brutal, humid August day at Inglewood the family had stood in the heavy floral sweetness of the air, and filed past through the clots of thin organ music beside the waxiness of death. Then Frank had gone east to his new job, and Marlene and Bob had returned to their homes, while Lon and his father trudged into the dead house at the beach that she had designed and helped build. They sat there alone in the empty rooms that echoed with stillness.

16

For a while, Lon had blamed his father, mostly for being too old to have a son fifteen. But after a year at Greyrock, he had realized grudgingly that Harold Renton had made an effort. That was the trouble again; he was too old to breathe life back into a dead house. The dishes stood stacked in the sink; the food hardened and spoiled; the dust thickened and staled until both of them knew it couldn't go on any longer. Lon had even welcomed the idea of Greyrock, where he imagined order and warmth —some sort of common sense. Otherwise why should they have a private school in the first place? For discipline and not for love? What kid, not knowing, could image that?

"If you think you're the only man here in that situation," Captain Dart had said briskly, "you're mistaken. Almost every man at Greyrock comes from a broken home, Cadet Renton, and don't you forget it, especially when you're feeling so sorry for yourself. If you can, I mean. Here at Greyrock you'll be busy from reveille to taps, starting right now."

Dart made a quick, impatient gesture toward Lon's suitcases.

"Your gear there—We don't throw it around in the fashion you've done at home all your life." He turned and tapped the desk behind him. "You'll find a list of room regulations in your Greyrock Manual in here. I want these quarters policed and ready for inspection—" He glanced at his own glittering gold wristwatch and stood. "—by two thirty. Attention!"

The captain had waited until Lon figured that he wanted him up on his feet too. So he had stood while that gruesome smile twisted Dart's face again.

17

"I'll assign Groot to these quarters," he said like a delicate whip flickering flies from a horse and barely touching skin. "We'll put Bates in with one of the Second Platooners. Oh, we'll make a Greyrock man of you, Cadet Renton. Don't you ever worry about that." He put his hand on the doorknob; then turned. "At ease," he'd said.

Ease.

Groot, as it turned out, was a huge blob of guy who had been at Greyrock four years with how many left to go nobody knew. Cecil Groot, III, was his full name, and nothing told the story of Captain Dart better than that he'd had to move out of Newman's room and in with Lon.

Newman was the only friend Groot ever had—at Greyrock or anywhere else. The two got along together because they had in common an impenetrable and invincible shield against the whole world: they were both so absolutely stupid that they shut out every sharp edge Greyrock used to slice a person into submission.

Plenty of times Lon had envied them both; they had a world of their own in which they could laugh together about nothing funny or lapse into an opaque daze that was as unassailable as a fishbowl. Although they both got every kind of dirty trick played on them by the other cadets, neither seemed to have the capacity for real anger. Lon suspected that Groot was too dumb to be anything except kind.

Once he had caught a mouse and kept it in a tin box he had hidden in his drawer where it could be heard at night, scratching frantically to get out. Groot fed it carefully and played with it for hours on his blanket, sometimes in the middle of the night when Lon was supposed to be sleeping. He was torturing the little animal, of

course, but Groot didn't know that. When the mouse died
—which it had to do sooner or later—he was gloomy for
days afterward as if he'd lost a friend he really loved.

Another sort of guy could pretend Groot's kind of
stupidity for a while and protect himself that way. Plenty
of them tried it. But Groot's fortress was a natural gift
within which nothing could hurt him much, not even
real physical pain like a hotfoot which he kept getting
because he could fall asleep almost anywhere. He'd wake
up, yowling in agony and jumping around on one foot
like a bear. But then he'd grin because he knew somebody
had noticed him, and walk around with the burnt end of
the match, showing it off with actual pride, a tendency
that took quite a bit of the fun out of the joke.

Lon had tried to take his side in the first week, calling
out a cadet named Olin Reese from the refectory for fill-
ing Groot's plate up with salt. Reese was a tough kid from
San Diego, cooler than ice and coordinated, and a lot more
than anyone needed to take on after dinner. He proved
it outside, belting Lon a couple of good ones, short, sharp,
and teeth-rattling.

"Why did you pick on Olin?" Groot wanted to know
that night after lights were out, his soft voice blobbing
in the darkness. "He's my friend."

So what was the use? Lon caught on right away to the
Greyrock style. He lied all the time about everything,
especially himself, and he observed the regulations scrupulously. It paid off. Just four days ago in Dart's office,
the captain had attested to that.

"Lieutenant Renton," he'd said, "I'm sorry to see you
go before your final year. I had you picked to command
the Corps next semester."

19

Lon's eyes had never even flickered. "Thank you, sir," he had replied with clipped modesty. "I'm sorry, too. I'll never forget Greyrock, or you, Captain Dart. You've done a lot for me."

"We've done what we could," the captain had answered, extending his hand and smiling that way for the last time. "Most of it was up to you, Lieutenant. You were Greyrock material in its very best sense."

Lies! Lies! Lies! They lied to you and you lied back to them. And if you weren't like Groot, absolutely unsinkable in your honest stupidity, they made you into their dirty little Corps Commander.

It was the way and Lon had learned it well. They did all they could to trap a person, but a cool head went along with them and waded through cheerfully, crawling and cheating for class grades, rank, off-campus leaves, and anything else around he thought he wanted enough to do the work for it. Greyrock? It was the whole world.

Morning bloomed in full sunlight and the bus passengers coughed painfully and ruffled themselves straight like caged birds with black ragged feathers. Voices murmured in conversation, cigarettes were lighted, and finally someone had the energy to laugh. Miserable or not, they were traveling; going there fast.

Lon glanced at the sailor across the aisle, while beside him Mr. Haley had begun to clear his throat in long, gargling reaches. The sailor was young. He sat erect, with his arms folded across his chest and his white cap squared and pushed down low on his forehead, thus shortening his already close-coupled face which was dark with the night's stubble and a darker ancestry. He was a little guy —one of those who are as tight as steel and who fear nothing at all.

"Well, boy," Mr. Haley said, opening the day's lecture, "you slept like a log. But I don't suppose you feel thankful that you're young enough to do that, heh?"

"I guess not," Lon murmured, scooping a phrase from the shallow, easy part of his mind.

The sailor had turned to shoot one glance of mild recognition in Haley's direction, the way campers regard a cloud of mosquitoes and accept them without anger or contempt but merely with annoyance. Suddenly Lon envied him his freedom. Someday—someday soon—

Mr. Haley cleared his throat once more. "When you're as old as I am, young fellow," he observed sagely, "you'll know a thing or two, maybe. Why, back when I was your age—seventeen, wasn't it—"

And so on and on—across Iowa and into Illinois, through the farms and villages, cities and towns, Mr. Haley held Lon Renton as a prisoner to his recollections and wise advice.

In all that distance he never suspected that Lon's brief and courteous answers were empty of meaning or attention, spoken as effortlessly as a machine spins at the touch of a switch, and were thus the essence of human contempt.

When Mr. Haley finally took his leave at the Chicago terminal, he was doubtless refreshed by that good adult sense of fulfillment for having turned a dreary trip to advantage by setting another young fool on right paths. In that vanity, he failed to notice that the sailor tossed him a gesture of amused farewell, while Lon's face was as expressionless as stone.

On a new bus headed north along Lake Michigan, Cadet Lieutenant Renton permitted himself to think again of Thelma and his father. Mr. Renton had wandered for months from Florida to Maine in a saga as irresponsible as anything kids ever did. But Marlene, Bob, and Frank had thought the whole second childhood as "good for Dad."

The man had at last returned to Milwaukee, where he'd gone to school in his youth and eventually worked upward in the sales and promotional departments of Englehart and Schmid, manufacturers of fine engineering instruments.

As he'd written to Marlene, he'd met the same Thelma Potter he'd known so long ago, still unmarried and teaching in the same kindergarten. He had asked her to be his wife.

Lon had read only parts of one letter. It was apologetic and almost pleading for understanding in a sickening way, he thought. But it had utterly delighted Marlene. She intended to keep it forever so that her two children would remember their grandfather for what he really was—"an intensely human individual, after all," as Marlene put it.

Lon had said nothing at all. But he knew that out from Greyrock the whole mess spun in swirls that cooled, thickened, and hardened the farther away a person searched. It wasn't to be put into words for his sister, who was more of a stranger to him than Captain Dart, or Groot.

Thelma's handwriting was like the samples in the books. In her note she'd said, "We want you to come home to us, Lon, dear. We have a big house that's old and comfortable, and your room is on the second floor near the stairs. My brother, Carlos, liked it especially because he could come in at night through the back door without disturbing anyone in the house." And a lot more.

Why did they think they had to lie, all of them from kindergarten teachers to bus passengers? He didn't know.

But he did know exactly what Thelma would be like, although they hadn't sent a picture—just the money and the ticket. She'd be tall to match his father, who was a big man already stooped from the burden of carrying his shell of gray plumpness. She'd be old and bony, with a strange childishness to her ideas, and a voice as stringy as cold chocolate syrup. She would play the piano in nursery tunes alternated with sick, romantic ballads—the old songs, the good ones, as she would call them. And she would tell all around the neighborhood about how "her boy, Lon" had come home to be with them now, and she was giving everything she possessed of womanhood in trying to be his mother.

He hated her already in the way he had hated Nebraska, Iowa, and the dirty confusion of Chicago. But Thelma didn't really matter and neither did they except as so many miles to travel, so many streets to cross through a jumble of stones, miles of steep roofs where people as faceless as dirt shunted through the cars, the brutal traffic, going nowhere, doing nothing.

Why, Thelma had never married in all those years! She had stayed in one school, marching the little kids around and around until his father had come back to trip her out of step. Lon wondered what a man could have to say to a dried-up woman after all those years that had ended in a handful of flowers one hot August day. Did he say, "It sure has been a long time, Thelma?" Or what?

The ride up the north shore lasted only a few hours. Wisconsin rolled in at once, green and pretty, if a person liked scenery enough to forget the grim towns, filthy with smoke.

Finally they dragged through south Milwaukee and at length reached the Greyhound terminal on Michigan where Lon carried his heavy suitcase, realizing at last how tired he was.

He looked around hurriedly, searching a hundred faces and shapes, and as he'd expected, his father wasn't there to meet him.

Lon shrugged elaborately to show himself that he couldn't care less, but abruptly it hit him again as it had so long ago in the dormitory—that terrible inward sickness from which he probably could never recover. It was a physical thing, catching at the muscles of his face and making his lips tremble.

In panic, before people began looking at him, he set down the suitcase right where it was and got into the rest room where dozens of men milled around within the moist, disinfected atmosphere. He quickly found an empty washbowl, turned the cold water on full, and slopped it heedlessly into his face and over his hair. With the paper towels he dried as much as he could, taking his time and combing his straight black hair.

He noticed again how much heavier his brows were than his features could use, and that his eyes were an offbeat hazel color set deep in bony shade so that they brooded darkly beneath hairy lashes.

His face was lean and matched a slightly aquiline nose, with an expressive, full-lipped seriousness to his mouth that hid crooked white teeth. Sometimes Lon saw in the mirror a lurking, dark man who was reckless, purposeful, and perhaps dangerous—but that was only a shadow.

Right now he saw something else more realistic, and blue. A cop, coming his way.

24

With studied calm, he replaced the comb in his pocket and pretended to find a spot on his chin worth special attention. The cop wasn't for him, naturally, but cops made him nervous.

Something touched his arm and drew ice.

"Son," said the heavy, phony voice, "are you named Lon Renton?"

"Yes," said Lon, turning slowly, his eyes clear and innocent behind their stainless steel. "Yes, sir!"

The cop's face was beefy, and thin red lines veined the lobes of his nose. His eyes were bright blue with suspicion.

"Good," he said. "Well, there's a lady out in the waiting room looking for somebody by that name." He grinned. "Know her?"

"Yes, sir," Lon said, smiling back. "She's my—" pausing so briefly that the words flowed without a perceptible break, "mother."

"Good!" said the cop again, pleased for the few little things in his work that sometimes turned out happily. "Fine!"

So Lon went outside and there was Thelma standing beside his suitcase. She was alone, and as Lon had imagined, she was tall, bony, and had iron-gray hair. He walked toward her slowly, wondering where his father could be and not knowing what to say. Then she noticed him, and smiling, stepped forward.

Long afterward, Lon was going to remember that her voice wasn't like cold chocolate syrup at all. It was— well, just a voice with a genuine note of gladness in it, as if—it didn't matter.

"You're Lon," she said, still smiling. "I'd know you anywhere because you look so much like your father." She reached out and took both his hands in hers, holding the pose that way a second while she met his glance directly. She had gray eyes as hard as his ever would be, but he didn't waver.

Instead, he waited for the kiss, dreading it but prepared. They blew a kid's nose in the kindergarten, washed his face, taught him a little song to fool his parents.

He was wrong; he felt only Thelma's eyes searching through his for something she seemed to recognize. Then she gave his hands a quick little squeeze and let go decently.

"I'm so glad you've come," she said. "Your father is at work and couldn't be here, and I"—she laughed lightly —"got caught in the traffic. I'm awfully sorry I was late."

The funny part was that it seemed to be true—she really was sorry. Glad, and sorry.

"I'm—" Lon began. "D-d-don't—"

He caught himself. Why, he'd started to stutter!

With fierce will, he forced himself to say it smoothly. "That's p-perfectly all right," he managed. "I know how someone can get tied up at the stoplights. Besides, I've been here only a couple of minutes—"

"Well—" she said, glancing at the big wall clock, "shall we go?"

"All right," he told her, picking up his suitcase.

She saw how it dragged down his arm. "I'm afraid that's going to be awfully heavy," she said. "The car is parked at least two blocks away."

"I can manage—" he replied, "ah—"

"I hope you'll call me Thelma," she said gravely, "and I'll call you Lon. Is that all right?"

"Yes," he told her. "Yes, ma'am."

26

2

MILWAUKEE WAS another city with the new plastered over the old in a style that left the seams showing. Like everywhere else, the downtown area was deteriorating. Storefronts stood empty or had been taken over by novelty shops and catchalls advertising cheap clothing. Skid row couldn't be far away.

Thelma's car fit Lon's picture exactly. It was a heavy sedan out of Detroit and old enough to be found in every automotive boneyard from coast to coast, but not the right year to be classic. When he put his suitcase in the scrupulously clean back seat he glanced at the speedometer and held a surprised whistle behind his lips. There were less than twenty thousand miles on this relic, which meant that its whole travel had probably been back and forth to the kindergarten with intermittent stops at the shopping centers.

"Would you care to drive?" Thelma asked, holding out the keys.

Once again Lon met those clear gray eyes and for an instant his own glance wavered, but he recovered immediately.

"No, thank you," he said at once without effort. "I don't know the streets."

She didn't argue. "All right, Lon," she replied, getting behind the old black wheel.

The car started to her touch and purred like a fat baby full of warm milk. It probably had been lubricated at every precise turn of a thousand miles, treated to the best mechanical care and never pushed.

He was surprised at the old girl's driving. Thelma didn't expect traffic miracles like most women; she had determination and was a good judge of distances. Also she revved up through the gears as if she intended going there the short way, but the pace was easy without squealing brakes and narrow escapes. He felt almost as relaxed as a motor vehicles driving inspector who has found one of the good ones toward the end of a nervous day.

He had to ask himself why she insisted on that phony request that he drive when it was the last thing she wanted or needed. She'd had sense enough not to slobber a fake kiss all over a total stranger when she met him in a public place, and to tell him at once that he could call her "Thelma" instead of "Mother." So why spoil it by making a show of trust? It was a sure giveaway that he'd be watched all the time.

Yet he reminded himself that she'd almost fooled him twice and he'd need to be careful with her because he had a weakness. Unless the person wore a uniform like a cop or Captain Dart, or sat behind a certain polished desk to show what he was, it took Lon time to figure some people. He guessed that it was because deep down he wanted them all to level and that was totally impossible. It made him squirm to say it even to himself, but he did.

28

"I wanted my stepmother to be my real mother."

He blotted that out instantly because it was stupid, and forced himself to concentrate on the traffic. They had passed through a district close to the lake and had now turned east on a street called Greenfield. Finally they were at an intersection with a four-lane boulevard.

"This is Twenty-seventh," Thelma said, gesturing with her bony arm. "Up in that direction a few blocks is Mitchell Park."

He glanced at the wide street, seeing nothing but the masses of cars bullying their way along. Mitchell Park was something big, to judge from her tone, but so was Wyoming and he'd seen that without too much panic. He waited to hear the glorious details—how lovely were the rhododendrons in the spring, how neat the sleet in winter. Captain Dart liked to give little nature talks too, especially to the new boys.

But Thelma didn't elaborate and Lon knew from that moment that she would always take a little extra figuring. Adults who were willing to allow a simple fact to stand alone in their talks with kids were rare. He began to feel uneasy in her presence because her silence begged for talk. When a guy forgot what he knew about adults even for a minute he was likely to fill in their empty spaces by saying the wrong thing at the wrong time.

He had a trick for silence that usually worked. It was to shut them out absolutely by asking yourself real questions about them. Then if a guy stared right into their eyes while he was thinking, a lot of them could become puzzled and anxious.

He started working on Thelma. Until his father had come along probably no one had ever been insane enough to ask her to marry him, because she was ugly and about as much woman as a grape stake. There had to be something really sinister wrong with his dad, or age had hit him with one of its destroying phases. Yet—

"Here we are," Thelma sang out. She pulled into a wide concrete drive at a corner lot. "This is our home."

For an instant, Lon sat there mute while he tried to say something right about a house—any house. There were the ordinary phrases a person learned to mumble about houses, but none of them suited this crazy place. It didn't belong in this world, and he struggled against an expression of what the structure really deserved—a shout of astonishment; maybe laughter. If a human habitation fit the householders, this was it. Here was a home that was truly one of a kind.

"It's probably different and strange to you, Lon," Thelma said, reading his mind again, "but it's comfortable and familiar to me. You see, I was born here—right up in that room above us, and so were my brothers, Carlos and Robbie. All this land around here—" gesturing, "all these city blocks were once part of my grandfather's farm. He built this house for my grandmother shortly before she died. The house was on a little knoll then, and the creek ran on down through a grove of magnificent maples that was right over there—" She pointed. "But do get your suitcase and come in. I want to show you your room."

Victorian—that was the house's design. It stood three full stories of frame and stone with a shell-shaped window of real stained glass on one side. The corner directly above Lon ended in a round turret with a conical roof that was like a castle lookout. Above was the steep slate roof angling into too many pitches to count. Below the foundation were concrete wells at ground level, showing the tops of barred glass windows which could lead to the dungeon, Lon supposed.

Lon couldn't help himself; he glanced at his stepmother with sympathy and understanding as he visualized her bent over the huge iron pot, stirring the mixture with the steering end of her broom while the one-eyed cat yowled in the background. Few guys could claim a witch in the family and it would likely be a distinction.

He hoisted his suitcase and followed her up the old stone stairs to the front door. It opened into a vestibule featuring a line of queer-shaped brass hooks on one side. A clothes stand of red polished wood stood at the end of that wall. On the other side was a long plate mirror and an umbrella stand of black-veined marble.

They went through the inner door, which was decorated with scrolls and carvings, to reach another hall leading straight ahead to massive sliding doors of light oak. These were closed, as were two other darker doors on the left.

On the right a carpeted staircase curved up the wall past the stained-glass window. This framed an alcove where reposed a three-foot replica of the *Venus de Milo*, as Thelma named it later on. The foot of the carved and curling banister sprouted a brass rod which supported a globe of green and blue leaded glass similar to that in the window.

"It's up here," Thelma said, pointing to the stairs. "Set your suitcase down on the landing and rest a moment."

He did as he was told and then waited. She had a reason, he guessed.

"This statue," said Thelma, "was a gift from your father. He gave it to me on my nineteenth birthday."

Lon stared.

"I see," he told her, nodding, and it was the truth. He saw, and nothing more.

The hallway above was wide enough to drive a Volkswagen through and almost long enough to run through the gears. It was paneled halfway up in wood, with the rest of the wall and ceiling papered. Wide carpeting ran past several doors that reminded him of an old dormitory. Two or three ancient light fixtures of brass hung down, but the main illumination came from a huge window at the end of the hall.

Thelma walked all the way to the window and opened the door of the last room, waiting there until Lon reached her.

"I thought this would be most comfortable for you," she told him, sounding uncertain for the first time. "The stairway there goes down to the service porch and the rear entrance. This door right across the hallway is the bathroom." She waited.

"It's fine," he said.

He put his suitcase in the middle of the room and turned to face her, seeing everything. There was a closet with hangers, a Greyrock-type bed under one window, the small desk and chair with a student lamp, and a large wooden chest of drawers. And one more thing: there was an enormous glass pitcher and basin, both milky white, standing on a triangular marble shelf in the corner. A small mirror was above it, with towels tucked in below. The walls were papered but otherwise undecorated.

She read his glance. "I—I didn't know you very well, Lon, except for what your father has told me. I thought you'd prefer to choose your own decorations later on."

Once again he met his stepmother's eyes and then saw the gadget behind her in the gray metal box attached high on the wall. It had three rows of little arrows, all pointing down.

"Anything you picked would be all right," he said absently.

"This was the maid's room back when our family had maids," Thelma said. "It was the custom then, you know—" She looked down, studying the rag carpet on the floor, a round job braided by hand either a long time ago, or yesterday. It was scarcely worn. "In each of the rooms," she went on, "there is a bell cord or a button. When one pushes the button, the little arrow for the corresponding room turns and a buzzer sounds. Or it once did. Some of the buttons still work, if you'd care to—to experiment." She laughed nervously. "You don't feel like the maid to be here, do you, Lon?"

He created a good smile—the kind they liked to see on a kid—and saw it reflected in her old eyes.

"No, of course not. It's a great room, and thanks for doing it just right."

"Are you hungry?" she asked seriously. "Or—I could fix you a nice snack right now if you like."

"No, thank you," he told her. "I—I ate before you came to the bus station. I'm not hungry at all."

"You're terribly tired though," reading truth, "and here I stand chattering. Why don't you take a nap right this minute and when you awaken you can eat?"

She said it like somebody's maiden aunt in the book who was always wanting to fill her boy up and never could because he had this hollow leg, as they liked to call it. Thelma looked as if she hadn't eaten a square meal in the last month.

"Sounds like a good idea," he admitted.

It was. When she was gone he went across the hall to

what she'd called the bathroom, a place big enough for a whole platoon of Greyrock cadets. The bathtub stood up high on iron claws, while the washstand had old hand-made brass fixtures built like eagles and the porcelain bowl was surrounded by more marble. The flush box was up out of sight at the top of the twelve-foot ceiling, with a zinc pipe running down the whole distance. Naturally there was no shower.

He took a tub bath in cold water because the hot had just begun to show up by the time everything was finished. It had to be at least a mile down to whatever they used for heating—candles, maybe, hand-dipped by Daniel Boone after the Peace of the Thirty-six Buffaloes.

He was asleep almost as soon as he hit the sack, but he had time to think of that foolish white statue down in the alcove and to see his father handing it to Thelma for her nineteenth birthday. In a way, it explained a lot of things. No wonder he was entirely alone and outside everything they did or thought or said.

He felt a kind of pity for Thelma and his father. She had married a statue, and Harold Renton had picked himself up a gray-haired kindergartner who still lived in the gingerbread house in the deep, dark maple woods where you could make a little arrow jiggle and get the maid on the double, day or night.

He awakened to discover the sun in his eyes from a different quarter, and when he saw the gray woolen blanket crumpled at the foot of the single bed, he thought he was back in Greyrock. Then he remembered and sat up.

A little later he washed his face in the basin where he'd found the pitcher full of water and heavy. He unpacked his suitcase, dressed, and went into the hall. From the stairwell he heard a murmur of voices and picked out his dad's. They were somewhere downstairs, and it was morning.

He knew he'd slept around the clock and he could picture that tall, skinny woman creeping upstairs through the night to listen and then report him still dead to the world. She was the kind who watched and worried a thing she'd set as her duty until it either hatched and flew away or died in the shell.

Lon felt his chin and went back to shave and comb his hair again. Satisfied, he took a deep breath and went down the stairs. At the bottom lay an enormous porch that seemed entirely empty, although there was an old Maytag washing machine and a wicker clothes hamper near some cement tubs. At the far end was a glass door, and outside was a monstrous back porch under a high roof supported by spindly wooden pillars.

The voices came through the door through which he could see his father and Thelma sitting at the checkered oilcloth spread of a kitchen table within. Harold Renton was speaking earnestly and lifting a coffee cup which spilled because his hand shook. He'd put on more weight, and his hair was almost white now, with only a little of the old-time black sprinkled in near the top.

Lon shrugged. It had to be sometime, so he opened the door and entered a kitchen that was a vast expanse of printed linoleum, old wooden sink, a refrigerator, and a great black stove big enough to fry a whole cow at once, or so it seemed.

The spaces in between these articles were like full-fledged hikes to eyes conditioned by the California housing tract style of a small kitchen that was a model of tight efficiency.

For a second he saw them for what they really were— lonely old people having trouble looking into each other's eyes and sitting in a barn of a kitchen where talk echoed.

Then Harold Renton saw him and set the cup down, spilling more coffee.

He stood up, a big hand held out. "Lon!" he puffed so that his soft, gray jowls trembled. "Why, Thelma, here's our boy at last. How are you, Lon?"

Lon took his father's hand, sensing its moisture and tension and knowing instantly what the man had found on his long search backward into the past. Nothing. Instead he'd lost his hold on everything else that had existed before. His father felt dead; death lingered in his gray skin and at the edges of his voice.

Harold Renton didn't know it. He slung a heavy arm around Lon's shoulder and pushed him over to the table.

"Sit down! Sit down!" he bellowed in that fake heartiness that fathers were supposed to have. "My, isn't it fine to have him, Thelma? Now we have our family with us."

Lon noticed that Thelma's eyes flickered with that strange inward light that gray eyes sometimes possessed. She knew that her husband's voice was phony, and she realized that the son had caught on right away, too. She was as sharp as broken glass and missed nothing, for which a guy had to give her credit.

But there was another quality. Thelma was crazy about his father—that was clear. With her he could do no wrong, and somehow she smiled in all that gloominess and it made her younger.

"My, yes, dear," she said. "But we'd better give Lon a chance to get settled before we—Oh, I'm forgetting. You must be famished, Lon. Here, start on this. I'm sure you'll like it."

From a teapot, she poured a thin, hot liquid into a cup at the place his father had forced him to occupy. It was set with a thick plate and heavy kitchen silver.

He stared at the stuff because he'd never seen anything like it, not even at Greyrock. It resembled clear soup, colored a faint yellowish tinge.

Thelma almost giggled.

"It's hot celery juice," she explained. "Haven't you ever tasted it? Oh, come on, Lon, do try it. It's ever so nourishing and full of good things, good for you. I drink it instead of coffee and I was hoping that you would too."

"Drink it!" whispered Harold Renton at his side. His voice had a special tone that Lon recognized instantly, but he had never before heard it from his father.

"Yes, sir!" he said and poured down the juice, rejecting in that moment and for all time the juice of the celery stalk.

"We still have our celery farm right outside of the city," Thelma said. "The boys work it. You see, after—after our mother died, Carlos and Robbie and our father built a house in the country and I stayed on here." She studied the tablecloth. "And—well, we use a lot of celery at our table."

"Yes, ma'am," Lon told her. He'd been right all along about her and he felt reassured. She'd almost fooled him, but a guy found out sooner or later that they were all alike. Plenty of celery juice.

The remainder of breakfast was fine—toast and eggs,

but no coffee. Thelma didn't believe in it, and what his father had been spilling was tea.

Afterward, they took him into the rest of the downstairs until Mr. Renton left for work.

There was a huge dining room with mirrors and a glittering glass chandelier over a long oak table with chairs to match. Adjoining was the family sitting room which looked more relaxed. In there were glass cases crammed with strange odds and ends like shell collections, arrowheads, music boxes, and other paraphernalia. There was even a small stuffed alligator. Each item had a story to it, Thelma declared, but she had the decency not to relate any of them now.

Beyond, through an archway, was a room with a bay window. It was furnished with a square piano, matching cabinets, and some delicate straight chairs. On the floor was a Persian rug and on the walls hung dingy paintings in ornate gold frames, with lampstands in the corners holding fringed lamps with brass and marble bases.

Joining this music room were two outer parlors that were nearly identical, each with a small sofa and a couple of chairs, quilted and fringed and as hard as rocks.

"Every room in the house has a fireplace except yours, Lon," Thelma said, pointing to the small grates, above which were marble mantles decorated with clocks and knobby glassware or porcelain statuettes.

Wherever they went their footsteps echoed to the high ceilings on the hardwood floors, until at last they reached the front entrance, where a briefcase was standing.

"I'll have to go now," said Mr. Renton. "Good-by, Lon," and turning, "good-by, Thelma, dear." He bent at the waist a little to peck a kiss to her faded cheek. Then he was gone and Lon heard a car starting out in the yard, one that could use work from the sound of it.

"Your father tries so hard," Thelma said as soon as the door closed. "He's such a good man, Lon. You must be terribly proud of him." She sounded as if she were trying to convince herself. "It's a shame he hasn't found a position more in keeping with—with his abilities and education—" Her voice died away like a gust of wind worn out from stirring the fallen autumn leaves.

Lon didn't tell her his real answer. Instead, "Oh, sure," he said in agreement, and that was all.

A father was either terribly real or terribly distant to a son, he supposed. He remembered a man who had once known the names of the stars and who had possessed a searching curiosity about everything that grew in the woods, swam in the streams, or flew.

Lon thought he could remember how as a very little boy he would go with his father and mother on what she called "sketching trips." She would find some small corner of California, sight it through a couple of cardboard squares, and then set up her campstool, sketching board, and box of colors. Gradually, a picture would emerge—he seemed to remember that. It captured the corner and held it still.

More than that, he recalled a huge, godlike figure—a towering, slim, laughing man who recognized trees by name and birds by their call. He could hunt a patch of wild flowers all around the rim of hills the way others chased bears and money—

And who was that? Lon didn't really know.

Nobody had the right to say that a man was one thing now, without starting in the beginning and telling the whole story—the good and bad of it all. It was painful to hate your father, to pity him, and to love him, too. No, sometimes the only way a son could protect himself from even having a father at all was to be indifferent toward him.

So Lon shrugged. "I guess," he finished.

3

AS HE stood beside Thelma, Lon suddenly felt like
one of those characters in the haunted house, the
Gothic novel, the television story of chill horror where
doom and foreboding hung over all the scenery and movement. But you knew the whole time that it didn't matter;
you could dial another channel.

"We can look at the upstairs rooms later on," Thelma
said in a different tone. "There's a lot to get used to here,
I suppose, unless you grew up in this house. Why, there
are more than a hundred windows. One hundred and
twelve, exactly—" She smiled. "Each Christmas I put a
candle in every one of them. Does that seem very odd to
you?"

"It's a lot of candles to watch," he admitted guardedly.

"My, yes," she agreed. "Well, why don't you look around
for yourself now? Or better yet, take the car and drive over
to Mitchell Park. It's closest. They have the most wonderful conservatory, and the new geodesic domes have been
built. The—the young people are always there, summer or
winter, and—" She seemed to flutter. "And from there you

can drive down Greenfield to Fourteenth. Your high school—"

He told her the truth. "I don't like to drive someone else's car. I might—"

"Nonsense," she interrupted. "You can't hurt my car, and I know you're a good driver. A teacher knows a few things about young people after a while. You'll be careful and responsible. Do you have a license?"

"Yes. But it's for California—"

"You'll need to apply quite soon for your Wisconsin permit, but it's valid for several days, I believe. Perhaps later on you can get a little—" She broke off.

She was going to say, "—car of your own" he knew, but a recollection of something like money or the invisible dangers of the road stopped her.

"I can walk," he said. "I've done a lot of walking," which was the truth. He'd walked, hitchhiked, snagged the freights that slowed to a crawl behind Greyrock as they bunched their diesel-powered muscles for the long grade up Cuesta Pass. The guys rode up as far as they liked and walked back, just to spend the time—although getting caught meant being restricted to campus for a couple of months.

Thelma wouldn't have it that way, however, so a while later he eased the sweet old Buick out of the yard and around the corner, where he could breathe again. Taking off from the first light, he automatically hit the throttle, planning to blow a little antique carbon out of that relic's throat. But he didn't.

Lon had his own principles built into him long ago by somebody he'd forgotten. However unsuspected they were, he abided by these. He didn't abuse a decent ma-

42

chine; he left the place where he'd been neater than he'd found it; he opened books, turned their pages, and read them as if they were spun of precious stuff even though they bored him. Things and places demanded no more of him than he of them and thus Lon was no vandal and no street hood.

He had sensed at once that Thelma's house was unique. The fringed lamps, the polished rosewood piano, the glassware and porcelain figurines, all belonged to each other in some unexplainable manner the way things in a museum belonged. In their own nutty way they were priceless and perhaps beautiful, and so was Thelma and this old automobile, showing the same loving care. But he couldn't have told another kid how he happened to know that, so he kept quiet.

He gentled the car down the streets and dutifully turned at the corner she'd indicated with a neatly penciled map drawn on a paper grocery bag. He supposed that Thelma would do everything that way, from squeezing the celery juice to wiping dust from his father's foolish statue.

He pictured the man staggering up that curved walk with a hundred pounds of carved marble under his arm and hollering, "I have brought you this statue, Thelma," tipping his straw hat, "for your nineteenth birthday. It will just fit in that alcove on your stairway." Thinking about it, Lon grinned for the first time since he had left Nebraska.

Ahead was the park. He cut right off the boulevard and parked the car on Pierce Street, noticing instantly what Thelma had meant. This park did have a difference; it wasn't dedicated to keeping off the grass but to getting on it; there were provisions for every type of recreation from dancing, boating, skating, and tennis to just walking around in a sweet place. Not bad, he had to admit, but he still felt aloof from it all, objective and detached because he really didn't want any part of it.

Then he saw Hermine Mannheim coming toward him on the walkway, and suddenly they were both alone in one of those random islands of silence which appear in the center of crowds.

Hermine was beautiful; there was no other way to describe her that didn't shamble off into a swamp of words. Yet her beauty wasn't the ordinary kind a guy had learned to expect. Lon's first reaction to her was almost dismissal—as if she fascinated and repelled him at the same time. Other living creatures had affected him in the same way—tigers and flamingos, for example. As it turned out, there might have been a little of each in Hermine.

She was smaller than most, dressed in loose summer cottons that hid her so much it showed her, walking strongly, looking younger and therefore vastly older than usual girls. Her dark hair was glossy and cut wild to frame an oval face, where features were made more delicate by a wide, full-lipped mouth.

Her eyes were large and wicked from too much knowing innocence; she looked out upon the world with an insolence as sweet and diffident as honey. She saw Lon and smiled at him as if he was already hers, but it was merely accident. She was really smiling at a silver kitten, a jeweled monkey, a golden bird freewheeling in the vast sky of her imagination.

She's ugly, he thought instantly. Wise, she thinks. Trying to be cute. Not over fourteen. Playing dolls in public.

Yet his lips gave back the smile. He slowed, stopped,

said, "This the way to the tennis courts?" Something stupid like that.

Rattlesnakes and wrens of amusement perched and coiled in her eyes, which slanted upward a trifle under eyebrows shaped to make them appear fine. Her quickened smile gave away a flash of white. She had a small scar on her neck which she realized he saw, perhaps because she wanted him to see it.

"You know it is. What else could those courts be?" Her voice was one part protective defiance and one part neighborhood girl, growing up cool, you see. There was another ingredient: something low and musical but seldom heard because it was nowhere over ages of nothing.

"That's right," he said. "Who could miss them?"

He waited to be put down hard, ready with a salty comeback. The women, now—a person could never trust them either. They tested their power by cruelty sometimes, and all you could do was shrug them off.

"I thought I knew you from school," she said. "I'm nearsighted and ought to wear my glasses, but I don't. You aren't a bit like him, anyway. You're more—"

"More what?"

She met his eyes with stunning frankness. "Good-looking," she told him easily. "Different in a funny way."

He didn't react to that because he didn't know how. It was a new approach.

"I'm Lon Renton," he told her instead, "from California. I'm supposed to be a senior next year at the high school on—"

"I'm a senior there, too," she replied. "My name is Hermine. Isn't that an awful name? Hermine Mannheim. I'm terribly German—"

"It's a pretty name. I never heard it before."

She laughed. "Neither has anyone else who isn't terribly German. Lon, you said. Is that for Alonzo or—or Lonadelphia, or something interesting like that? Don't parents do sickening things in naming their children?"

"It's just Lon," he said, feeling stupid and awkward for no reason. "What do you mean, terribly German?"

She started to explain and that was how they happened to get into Thelma's car and drive and drive—through Juneau Park along Memorial Drive and out through a place with many apartment houses called Shorewood, and beyond to Whitefish Bay. There in the nice suburbs the houses took on California lines after all. He learned more about Hermine in that short time than he knew about all the other people in his life combined.

She liked to dance, swim, and skate; she had a talent for art and wanted to go on to the Layton School of Art after graduation, but she didn't think she would. Her parents thought that high school was enough education for a girl.

Hermine was the youngest of three and the last left at home, but far and away the worst, most difficult, most thoroughly spoiled. Her mother still made at least thirty kinds of cookies for the Christmas holidays and kept doilies on the furniture. Her father was infinitely worse, being the German within the German as she described the condition, making an upward motion to show how his neck fit his head and laughing in delight at her own antics.

"You will do this; you will do that," she shrieked out into the air at all the people going by. "That's how he talks. And it's terrible, because he believes himself."

Then she stamped her feet around on the floorboards

46

to show how her father stamped around the house, dis-pleased, truly vexed, blowing out his cheeks, and bringing order to a mad, mad place.

"Most of the time I feel like screaming," she confided. "I think I can't stand them, either one. But I laugh instead; they're so funny and I really love them so very, very much."

In Milwaukee, she said, there were the Poles and the Germans—although the Association of Commerce liked to add Austrians, Russians, Italians, Irish, Jews, Scandi-navians, Swiss, Slovaks, and Negroes "mixed in." The Poles predominated on the south side and had resisted the influx of other groups.

"They say that somebody speaks 'a beautiful German,'" she told him. "They still say it—" She made a pompous face with her own cheeks blown out and rattled off a string of *ich, bist, dich,* sounds, and shrieked again with laughter at her own mimicry. "If I go out with a boy"— putting her hand over her mouth first and then saying in a strange little voice—"I go out with boys all the time. I have ever since I was fourteen. Do you mind?"

"No," he lied. He minded a lot. And if they all got to know her as easily as this, why, it meant that she—

"It doesn't mean that I've gone—" She appeared to rock in the seat a moment while she twisted her hands together in her lap. "I haven't been—been in love with any of them," she finished. "Do you believe that?"

"Yes," he told her, lying again. "So finish your story. I mean about the boy—"

"Oh—" smiling her odd inward smile once more. "Well, I say, 'Papa'—I call him that because he likes me to—I say, 'Papa, I was out with the nicest boy last night at the high school dance. He speaks the most beautiful Polish you ever heard. He says his mother insists he speak it at home because she wants the rich old culture preserved. The culture of the motherland must be preserved, Mrs. Lubienski tells Tommy.' "

"Then what happens?" Lon asked.

"It's mean of me, I suppose," Hermine said, staring at the floor in contrition. "I know that but I can't help it. Poor Papa will begin to stamp around on the heat register. We still have those because our house isn't very modern. 'Mrs. Who?' he'll finally say. 'That crazy Lubienski woman?' He says it in a hoarse whisper so the neighbors can't hear. My parents are very conscious of the neighbors. Anyway, 'You went to a dance with that foolish Lubienski kid,' he'll whisper, 'and he's—he's keeping up the—the Polish—you said culture, didn't you?' "

"I say, 'The old culture, Papa,' because I love to tease him. I say, 'The white kind when they had all those big horses and nice czars in Poland. The kind our history teacher tells us about when he says that Warsaw and Krakow used to be the real intellectual centers of—' "

" 'Stop right there,' he'll yell, forgetting all about whispering. Poor Daddy—" Hermine finished wistfully. "He so wants to bring a girl up right and he tries so hard, but neither he nor Mamma has any idea how—"

"Don't your sisters help?" Lon inquired.

Hermine giggled. "They're both married and away. You should know my next sister, Hilda, Lon. The oldest one is named Eva. Hilda was a terrible mess until she got married and raised some kids of her own. The Poles and the Germans are very proud in Milwaukee, but the kids don't care at all, even though their parents do. Now Hilda is starting to talk like Papa. She named one Helmuth and the other Eric. I mean, her boys. They're twins, only two years old, isn't that silly?"

"Yes," Lon said, because it was.

She laughed as if she had honey in her blood. "They all say I'm 'difficult.' Miss Coblentz sent a note home once that said it; she's dean of girls. 'Hermine is a difficult girl and very uncommunicative,' she said. Whenever Papa is really mad at me he says I'm difficult and uncommunicative. Do you think I am, Lon? Do you think I'm uncommunicative?"

He grinned down at her. "No," he said, "not if a person listens."

She turned toward him explosively, pointing her tapered finger. "That's it," she cried. "You listen. You're the kind who listens and I knew it right away as soon as I saw you."

"I talk, too," Lon told her.

"Say something now. Tell me about California and Hollywood."

"Sometime I will."

"When?"

"Tomorrow."

They had headed back along Memorial Drive and the road had reached a little cove with a turnoff and railing above the rocky shore of Lake Michigan, blue in the afternoon sunshine. Far out toward the water's horizon a white-hulled car ferry steamed eastward. He stopped the car and turned to the girl, searching her eyes for something but not knowing what he sought.

Although the traffic hummed by only a few feet away, she came into his arms without hesitation and her kiss was stunning to Lon. It was—almost savage and fierce,

49

as if Hermine were hungry for a boy's arms and his kiss. Her small body, leaning into his, was unexpectedly strong and thrusting, as if charged with warm lightning and energy.

Afterward they sat apart again and watched the lake in silence. Lon said nothing at all. It was only a kiss.

Finally, "I suppose you think I kiss every boy I meet that way," Hermine said in a faraway voice, "because I told you how much I go out with them. I suppose you think I throw myself at any boy I happen to meet in the park."

He did, naturally, so he picked his reply with caution. "Does it make a lot of difference?" he asked. "I mean, is it really better to be German than Polish?"

"Yes," Hermine said.

"Better, you mean?"

"No. I mean it makes a difference."

"Why?"

She turned away so that he could see only the back of her head, still glossy and wild—but different now. She looked fragile again, even forlorn.

"Because I love you," she said in a sudden voice, turning quickly and catching his stare. "I know I do"— motioning with both hands, fingers extended and spread open. "Oh, not all at once like that kiss thrown at you. We've only known each other a couple of hours. I mean that much: a couple of hours of love. I know we fit somehow and that you're not like any boy I ever met before"—and here she smiled in a secret way of her own—"and I'm not like any girl you've known. We're different because we belong to each other, and we've been waiting around all this time to meet. Do you think I'm stupid?"

"Why—why, of course not!"

50

"Yes you do," she said, half teasing and half serious. "Because you think I kiss every boy I meet the way I kissed you—right out on a public highway in front of everyone. You think I don't care anything—anything—But I want to tell you I've never kissed anyone that way before. You can believe me if you want. You can believe anything you like."

"All right," he said.

He swung the car back into the traffic and headed toward Greenfield.

After a while, she said very softly, "Tell me about California, Lon."

Slowly on that ride, Lon discovered that he wasn't alone anymore. There were two people here in this special outer edge of the world—Hermine and himself. And he learned a couple of other things. She liked to listen better than she talked, and he discovered an unsuspected eloquence of his own.

California, he said, was a place where the snow on the mountains lay blue-white against the lilac sky. The slopes dipped down through lemon groves so emerald green that lively persons traveled miles just to see them slide. The orange trees beside the sparkling cities grew in endless weed-bare rows of wheeling lines of rich brown soil, perfectly patterned for miles and miles and sometimes in heavy blossom beside branches of full-term fruit.

And Los Angeles? Why, it was a great, beautiful city where square miles of neon at night glittered like an Aztec lake of jewels. At night the moon hung like candy in the velvety sky, and there were uncounted wonders to see and places to go with new ones built every day of shining stuff behind one's back. It was Disneyland and Knott's Berry Farm all over, with the people famous and as common as an old Corvette. Why, a person might meet Frank Sinatra in the parking lot where the old master could open a hard, brilliant song of a kid's own time. Kim Novak, Sammy Davis, Jr., or Bob Dylan and Joan Baez—anyone at all might come walking down your street as naturally as water flows.

It was the truth, because that was how Hermine wanted California to be—a long, long way from Milwaukee and the facts. It wasn't German, and it wasn't of this world. It was a great, lovely lie, and she listened almost in total silence the whole way home.

Yet Hermine had told him the truth. Her house was just as she had described it—old, steep-roofed, and huddled with the others. At the corner of Greenfield was Mannheim's Market. The woman standing on the house porch had to be her mother, plump and still pretty in a mother's style, if a person wanted to see that.

"I want you to come up and meet my mother," Hermine said.

"No. Not now."

"Please!"

So he went up on the wooden porch and stood around for a minute. Mrs. Mannheim didn't seem fierce at all. Instead, she acted gentle and worried.

"Please come in," she said. "My, my. All the way from California."

Hermine went back down with him to the car.

"Will you?" she asked, her beautiful face squinted into the sun.

"Will I—what?"

"Come back tomorrow?"

She meant it—that way. Asking him.

52

"Naturally," he said. "That is, if you'll let me. What time?"

"In the evening. Seven thirty or eight. We can go to the park and dance, or—They have dances there in summer. Or we can go boating on the lake. Whatever you like."

"I'll be here," he said. Then he froze, remembering something. "I—I might not have this car. I don't—"

"We can walk," said Hermine. "Or take a bus. I'd rather walk with you than ride in the best car in—in Germany."

"I'll be here," promising. "And thanks, Hermine, for—for letting me know you."

She became very grave, solemn, and serious. "Did you believe me about—about that?"

He had to think.

"Yes," he said because he did believe her.

4

HE DROVE toward Thelma's house down streets paved with wonder, where all the people were habitants of a friendly, relevant world. They had built this city, seeded the grass in the park, and held it all together until the one miraculous moment unfolded and Hermine walked into his life.

Not really, of course. But he did have her kiss still lingering with him like a fragrance, and she had given him tomorrow. It had been years since he'd possessed a day like that. He could almost feel it in his hands.

She'd said, "I love you," as if it were a plain fact known all along to them both. In his whole life he'd never heard the words before. Not like that.

He tested them now in the traffic ahead. "I love you," he told the blank rear deck of a late sedan. It came out as a hoarse whisper in an unnatural tongue, so that he knew he had never used the words himself—except maybe when he was a little kid and they'd meant something else entirely.

And how about that first impulse of his? Ugly, he'd called her, wise! A smart little kid playing games. He'd nearly walked away from the loveliest thing that had ever happened to him. She hadn't said one word or made a single gesture he could have predicted, yet she understood who he was and why he was here without asking a single question.

Beautiful—a girl—German, she had said. But she was a lot more than a pattern. She was a thousand intricate threads shimmering in a rope of silk, or she was quicksilver fractured to a million droplets of light when the boy broke the laboratory bottle.

Her bright chatter had run and skipped along like a California creek after the winter rains, now clear and full of purified sunlight, pools of swirled shadow, pebbles polished to amethyst dawns and ruby afternoons.

She made sense; she said who she was the way the creek told its name. Hermine was the tremulous sensitive silver grains of Lon Renton turned backward into the negative so that where she was gay and light, in him the darkness stood. Whatever she hid he carried outwardly and each was indispensable to the other because incomplete alone.

Let the adults say there was no such lasting emotion as love begun at first sight. They didn't know Hermine, and Lon. Nobody did.

The corner showed Thelma's house towering above the rest, and seeing it he felt something of his old fear. There were plenty of boys in Hermine's life, she'd admitted, and a person had to believe that. She was a girl to catch them all—rugged, tough, on the make, those looking for whatever was in it for them the easiest way. He knew the type too well and had often wondered why they managed. With him today, it could have been a game Hermine liked to play on an afternoon in the park when she happened to be bored.

He'd been around the girls a few times and nothing happened; not really. No magic; no miracle similar to this afternoon. He'd even kissed a few, goofed around in their presence at the beach and other places, or handed them here and there in a studied imitation of the perfect Greyrock cadet scrupulously following the rules for social occasions. Whatever he did, it always came out the same. There was an invisible wall between him and a girl that Hermine had known how to dissolve in an instant.

He had barely been able to talk with other girls about anything because their inclinations worked on records, dances, game scores, latest blasts. From them, Lon had learned how offbeat he was because he didn't belong to their world either. Sure, he knew the names of the musical combos, how the teams shaped up, the style of everything and the words to fit. He could tell how cool, how square, the moment was supposed to be. But he didn't really care to be that young.

He'd heard the girls' view of what he was. Susan Cokely said he was terribly shy; Robina Rawlins thought him snobbish. But Carol Rhigetti had been honest; she told all of Greyrock that he was stupid, and he'd believed Carol most because she was tall, blond, raucous, and stupid herself, so she probably knew best.

But could a guy tell the girls that it didn't matter to him? How could he say that the hatred, vengeance, cruelty, hooks, and lies that lay waiting for him were right in the room all the time? Who won, who lost, meant nothing because the Lon Rentons always lost anyway.

Subjects at school, teachers, styles, and modes were all the same parts of every hour in the long day where winning was like flies conquering flypaper.

How could a guy say to a woman with hair as stiff as cardboard that the whole sky pressed down with an intolerable weight and if you looked for a hole where you could stand up free, they'd slap you before the notion spread to anyone else? Did any girl know what it meant to wake up afraid, fear all day, and go to bed in terror? That was a game without any score at all.

So he'd been shy, snobbish, stupid, and kept quiet while he watched the regulations, studied the books, and repeated all the specious lies with such precision that next year he would have been the Corps Commander. Then he would have ranked with the women all right, as top monkey voted the Greyrock cadet most likely to succeed.

In one hour, Hermine had swept that all away like dust. Lon Renton marveled all the way home.

Home, he'd called it. Until he'd switched off the Buick's engine and glanced toward that crazy house he hadn't admitted to himself how late he was. Thelma and his dad were in there; he could see their shadows move and visualize their anger before he looked into their faces.

Adults had their time clocks wound and set; it was more important to them than blood, perhaps, because time was progress, work, money, and value. He had deliberately trained himself to that ritual until they had written into the record, "Lieutenant Renton shows an unusual sense of duty and responsibility."

This afternoon, he and Hermine had spilled away time like pennies through their spread fingers.

He knew what now: it was after six; dinner had cooled at the table and the celery had gone limp. By midafternoon, Thelma had begun to worry—not about her old car, mind you, but about the safety of "her boy." Finally, mild worry had become real suffering as she strained her ears toward every familiar engine noise. And what was responsible? Why, nothing but teen-age carelessness and inconsideration. Lon had heard it all before.

Therefore, he went inside like a Greyrock man, all resolute, contrite, and ready to take his punishment in the honorable tradition of fifty years of the corps before him— if anyone could imagine succeeding generations of parents sending their sons back for the same experience.

Well, he found out it was going to be different in Thelma's house.

"Lon," she said, her eyes actually lighting up, "did you have fun? Sit here at the kitchen table and tell me all about it."

"Hello, Lon," his father remarked. That was all.

She hadn't waited dinner. Instead, it was set back on the stove and she served his plate in the kitchen without any special celebration of what a heel he was for not getting the stuff piping hot.

His father went into the family living room. Thelma stayed in the kitchen and sat down opposite him with a cup of tea, where she watched him in silence.

"Did you go to the park?" she asked finally. "Or—"

"Yes," he replied. "You were right. It's a great park. I know why you pointed it out."

She liked that. Thelma was proud of the park; maybe of the whole city of Milwaukee.

"This is good," he added, meaning the food. It was a stew with a good flavor.

He ate hungrily, remembering that he had never once mentioned lunch to Hermine, a mistake he worried about for a second and then forgot. If she'd wanted something,

59

a hamburger or whatever, she was the kind to say so. He knew her that well already, and it pleased him that she'd forgotten too.

"I drove your car farther than you expected, I guess. I drove all the way across town above a place called White-fish Bay—"

"That's all right," his stepmother said easily. "I told you to take the car."

He inched forward, sparring. "I didn't put any gas in the tank, although I have quite a bit of money left over."

"I keep the tank full," Thelma said.

He lowered his eyes. Nobody was going to fool her on the first day with anything less than the absolute truth.

"I met somebody in the park," he said in a low voice. "We rode around and I forgot all about the time. That's why I was late. I'm sorry."

"Of course," Thelma answered. "It's quite all right, Lon. Later on we'll decide on a few easy rules about things like dinner and so on in order that we don't misunderstand each other, shall we?"

"Fine," he said, meaning it because he was relieved. Rules were the simplest part of their code. For a moment he'd thought she had him, because it was pleasing them freehand that would be really tough.

She smiled in a friendly way, and later he would remember that he might have trusted Thelma from the start, rules or no rules. She was as far-out as anyone could get, including himself.

Also, she was as hard as stainless steel in her peculiar virtue, which happened to be truth. Why, if the whole world had been like Thelma, it would have to be a place where the books were at least partly right.

60

"Who was the girl?" she asked.

He glanced at her, surprised. "How did you know it was a girl?"

"Easy—" she said, almost teasing him before she remembered her position. "I really didn't know. I guessed."

He almost created a name—like Susan Jo Harlan, or Candy Wellborn. They probably named girls the same stupid things in Milwaukee or anywhere.

"Hermine Mannheim," he said. "Happen to know her?"

Her thin eyelids blinked down; she knew Hermine. She knew of her. "Yes."

He waited.

"I know many of the young people in the district," she explained, glancing away, "and they know me."

He leaned forward, drawn toward his stepmother by a new bond.

"They know me mostly by reputation," said Thelma in a bland tone, but somehow making it seem firmer than that.

He didn't like the feeling he got that he'd missed a point cut very fine. So he said nothing.

"Hermine was one of the children I had in class," said Thelma, seeming to look back and sort through a host of children. "She was even prettier then—a little elf and terribly bright—the kind of child a kindergarten teacher will always remember—"

Lon scarcely ever interrupted an adult but he did now.

"You said they know you by reputation"—keeping his eyes down. "What sort? I mean, what do the kids think of you?"

She laughed. "That I'm tall, skinny, old, and strict, Lon. Very strict. That I'm a teacher and that I once took flying lessons and earned a pilot's license—which makes me very eccentric, especially at my age—"

He knew he'd scored. "But that's wrong, isn't it?" he said. "I mean, that isn't enough to know about any human being."

Thelma was thoughtful for an instant; then she stood up and took his plate quietly.

"You're a nice boy, Lon," she said from the sink, "and very intelligent. I'm sure we're going to become good friends. So next time you're going to be late, will you telephone and explain? You see, I'm used to that. Carlos and Robbie, my brothers, went wherever they wished—but they always let us know in advance and I grew accustomed to that."

"I certainly will," Lon told her, sensing justice and liking its warm glow.

"It's a bargain," Thelma answered. That was all there was to forgetting time and knowing a girl by reputation.

Shortly afterward, Lon went up to his room and hit the sack immediately. He wanted to think out a day in Milwaukee because if it went on like this every day, he was going to need changes in his attitude. Maybe Thelma wasn't much as a woman, but as a person she was close to being awfully human. And taking that, along with Hermine, wasn't going to be—

He heard steps padding up the stairs and a hand fumbling at his door. There was a short knock and his father entered.

"Lon," said Harold Renton into the darkness.

"I'm in bed. I'll snap on the light."

He did.

"Sit down?" he asked.

"No. This will only take a minute."

It took hours; it took all night; it took dreams.

Lon listened; he let him say it over again in ten different ways. Nothing was working out very well, his father declared. A son as young as Lon couldn't understand but he deserved the chance. Second marriages were difficult enough, and between him and Thelma there existed a period of "delicate adjustments" of many things.

In addition, or on top of all the burdens, there was the undeniable truth that a man's earning powers declined with age. A son as young as Lon couldn't understand the problem of keeping up a great barn of a house like this, and was in fact not expected to understand. They had asked him to come here and live because he was their boy and they both loved him and hoped that he would finish school as his wonderful sister and brothers had done in days gone by.

So be it. They were snug in their beds so to speak, and by way of saying. But the car was a different matter. It was Thelma's special car and even Carlos and Robbie had a particular regard for that lumbering, ungainly machine. It was in a sense a car that was more than a car and to dent or damage it would be unthinkable. Also dinner. Thelma had a special regard for dinner, believing that all should sit down together by candlelight and eat then and not later, nor in short orders.

Did he understand? Was the meaning, given in friendly, man-to-man language quite clear? The car was to be borrowed but seldom, and brought back on time. He must always have a care and be forever courteous to Thelma, helping with the little chores and continually remembering that she didn't understand teen-agers and probably never would because she had borne no sons, whereas he, Harold Renton, had endured an endless procession of sons, which now might at last terminate.

Through it all, Lon said nothing. It meant, really, that he wasn't going to have the car tomorrow night. In California, he recalled, if a kid didn't have a car, he probably didn't have a girl and the same thing was no doubt true in Milwaukee, no matter what Hermine had said.

He sat up angry, ready to tell his father the truth—that Thelma had practically forced the car on him, and—

But as Harold Renton talked on, his emotion left him in the face of something larger. This was his own father saying these ridiculous things. Why—why, he didn't know Thelma at all. He couldn't. After months together they were still total strangers to each other.

"You understand, don't you, Lon?" the man finished.

"Yes, Dad," he said. "I won't ask for the car. Don't worry."

His father reached the door and faced around again. "You see," he seemed to plead, "I need your help now. We all have to work at this together."

"Sure, Dad."

The door closed and the footsteps followed themselves up the long hallway until the sound disappeared into silence. Lon heard his watch rustling again as it had done that day at Greyrock. He got up and snapped off the light. Then he lay for a long time staring up where black bugs of darkness swarmed and swarmed.

The next day was a long time between sunrise and evening. Lon stayed aloof and silent until he was left alone.

By now he had stopped worrying about his father and

faced a more immediate problem. Without a car, yester-day's golden alchemy had become a leaden weight until he cringed when he imagined himself going to her door and trying to make a joke of her willingness to walk.

More than once, he came near to phoning her with an excuse, plucking her number at the dial until he saw her again beside him and set the receiver back in its cradle. He'd learn tonight, he guessed, once and for all about the kind of girl she was.

At the dinner table that night he told them he was going out to a show. Then he waited for objections.

"Would you like to take the car?" Thelma asked. "I don't think that your father and I—"

"No," he said. "No, thank you. I'll grab that Greenfield bus."

"Are you sure, Lon?"

"Or how about—" his father began.

"No," Lon interrupted. "The bus is fine."

He picked up his expression and smiled at them both. "Maybe some other time—a special occasion, say. I'll ask for the car then."

That satisfied her. "Yes. On a special occasion," she told him.

The night was warm and he took his coat off on the bus because his suit was heavier than the weather. At the right corner, he got off and put his coat back on, pushing him-self forward toward her house. He probably had never met Hermine, he thought. Perhaps there wasn't a Milwaukee.

Here were the stairs and the house. He moved up them to the porch and found the doorbell, which rang to his touch. It buzzed soddenly inside, and there was a moment of stillness, as if nobody lived here at all.

Then he heard the light, quick footsteps.

"Lon," she said, swinging the door open. "I'm so glad—" catching herself and half turning. "Please come in. I want you to meet—"

"Hermine," he whispered, "I couldn't get the car, and—"

"Come in," she commanded again, and he could see how her face glowed in lamplight. "Papa—" calling as Lon stepped inside, "Papa, this is Lon Renton. Lon, this is my father."

Greyrock training helped. "How do you do, sir," Lon said with exactly the right tone of respect. Mr. Mannheim looked a little bit like Hermine's mother—not so tough. Instead he was short and stout, with clipped gray hair and a tired manner.

"Good evening," he said briefly.

Lon noticed Mrs. Mannheim. She was sitting in one of the overstuffed chairs of the old-fashioned room; she had just laid down some needlework.

"Good evening, Mrs. Mannheim," he told her.

"Lon is Miss Potter's—uh—Miss Potter is Lon's stepmother, Papa," said Hermine. "Or should I say, Mrs. Renton—You know, the teacher—"

"Yes, I know Miss Potter," Mr. Mannheim nodded, smiling faintly.

"Well, we'll go now, Mamma," Hermine told them both. "All right?"

Her mother nodded but not until she had glanced at Mr. Mannheim and read his pale-blue eyes. "Don't be too late, Hermine," she cautioned, picked up her work again as if the matter were settled.

Out on the sidewalk, Lon looked down at her. She seemed even smaller than he remembered. "I don't have a car—" he said again, giving her every chance she needed.

She laughed softly. "Do you know something?" she said, low-voiced. "You were late? It got to be eight and then after, and I thought—"

"What did you think?"

She laughed again. "If you don't know, I won't tell you. Shall we—"

"Do you want to ride a bus?" he asked seriously. "Or—"

"No. Let's walk," she said. "It's more fun."

Hermine looped her arm through his and pulled herself against him close in a way that was almost that of a child, yet terribly mature. In time he was going to learn that it was her manner of showing absolute possession.

"Come on," she said. "It's this way down the street and across up there. We can walk down as far as National and—Oh, I'll show you the way as we go along—"

They walked a whole block in silence and suddenly Lon stopped. He remembered that he'd almost phoned this girl to say he wouldn't be here with her.

"What did you think when I didn't get there?" he demanded.

Her eyes were upturned toward him, lustrous in her small, serious face. "I was afraid you weren't coming," she said simply.

"Afraid?"

"Yes. Do you believe me?"

In a quick gesture, Lon kissed her lightly and then took her hand.

"Believe you?" he said wonderingly as they walked past dark houses where people sat on their porches and talked in whispers as if they were an integral part of darkness. "It's more than that. It's that I feel—"

He searched for words, finding too many to choose from.

"I know how you feel," she said. "You don't feel lonely anymore. Isn't that so?"

"Yes. How did you know?"

"Guess—"

"I can't. How?"

She giggled like silver.

"Mind reading. Hermine Mannheim the Great knows your secret."

He shrugged. "All right. But it's true. That's how I feel."

"I know," she said.

They were at a curb, waiting for a car to pass.

"I will tell you after all," she said. "It's because I feel the same way. I'm not lonely anymore, either. As if—" her eyes grew shadowed in the headlights' glare and her words haunted her lips in light and shade, "as if we would always be lonely unless we knew each other."

"Yes," he said, "that's true," because it was.

Measured in blocks and miles, it was a long way to the park. But that evening went by in a shower of sparks for Lon. One minute they were setting out and the next he had brought her home again, with the lake and the music all separate memories.

"Tomorrow?" he asked her.

"Yes."

"When? In the evening like this?"

"No. That's too long to wait. Tomorrow afternoon."

"All right."

He kissed her.

"I love you," he said.

68

"I know," Hermine told him, smiling to herself in some mystic way while her eyes glistened as if love were really half-sad. "I love you too, Lon," she whispered as if it were part of an old story set to slow music.

He walked home and there were a billion stars over Milwaukee while the city spoke its own dark language, crying a muffled siren wail against the grumbling complaint of distant traffic going somewhere unknown. Lonely sounds.

But Lon Renton didn't hear that. Instead, he heard the exultant joy of his own heart.

5

THE FALL came to Wisconsin this year with all its beguiling contradictions. The leaves turned; winter seemed to be waiting just below the surface of the earth; the lakes sometimes had a gray, somber look as they reflected the scudding clouds, but then they reasserted their charming blue, although their levels were reduced.

All around was the feel of deception, a teasing, half-melancholy reminder that today could be only a mirage. And in this strange season, Lon found it difficult to believe what was happening to him. The occasional chill breeze rippling the maples seemed only a modest accident where summer stayed the whole year long. But he knew that winter wasn't far off, although he had little conception of what it was really like.

Hermine meant what she said about love—although more than once he had been anxious in her presence, as if he might wake up and discover her gone like the afterglow of Indian summer.

Love had enough magic; knowing that girl had brought a reassurance that was new to Lon. He'd finally assembled

71

everything he was into an orderly pattern within which he took a new view. It was unbelievable, but after the depths of Greyrock, life had taken a turn that was sheer luck—enough to make him think that perhaps every guy got a lucky break at some time or other. He hoped so.

First it had been only Hermine, and from there Lon's world expanded outwardly. He couldn't call himself a loner anymore. There were plenty of others now, guys like Bo and Dick, Starky, friends—In one sense the whole high school belonged to both Lon and Hermine because the other kids talked of them together. They'd say, "Let's ask Hermine and Lon to go out to Lincoln Park—" or wherever the action happened to be.

That was only a detail, sure, but it was big for Lon. A guy set himself down in a foreign city and went to a high school built like an office building, yet it had to be home.

This morning in September, Lon walked down Mitchell toward that school, but more especially toward a certain corner. Waiting for him there would be Hermine, or if she happened to be a little late, it would be the other way around; he'd wait for her.

Right now he was with Bo Kalinsky and Dick Demuth, but Starky wasn't along. They were guys his own age he'd met in the neighborhood and they were all right.

Bo was a tall, pale character with a thin smile and hair so white you could see his pink scalp through it. Dick was shorter and had an engaging, pleasant style. Along with Starky, they were in a kind of club or gang that had its undefined headquarters around the Greenfield playground, which was west of Thelma's house.

The Greenfields, as they called themselves for lack of

any definitive name, were loosely organized and not like some of the other gangs that wore distinguishing jackets with an insigne or symbol.

The Greenfields played sandlot ball together and did plenty of talking about money, school, and women. The existence of other gangs was really their sole unifying force; it gave them a sense of protection, maybe, from a genuine bunch like the "K's," who wore the name, a white K, on a black triangle. It had taken Lon a while to understand them because there had been no real counterpart of the Greenfields in his California experience.

They'd accepted Lon without question, as if being the same age and living in the neighborhood were ample credentials, especially after he'd demonstrated a considerable skill learned on the Greyrock billiard table.

As individuals they emerged with much greater clarity. Bo Kalinsky's ambition was to get out of high school as soon as possible and go to work with a cabinetmaker as apprentice. He wanted to escape the restrictions of his home, yet cabinetmaking was his father's trade and Bo admired the old man's craftsmanship.

"They tell me when to get in at night and when to get up in the morning," Bo would say of his parents. "I can't stand it. They nag all the time. I'm lazy, see; I'm worth nothing. It's like that all the time."

Demuth's main subject was girls. He talked about them constantly and what he said wasn't too flattering. Girls were like things in his mind, and Lon had noticed that the women in the neighborhood already knew that.

"Let's go out to West Allis," he'd say. "They've got better women. Around here, they're all ugly and egotistical."

He talked about every girl he'd gone out with in the same way—except for one: Hermine. Of her he merely said, "Renton, you got yourself a real woman there."

Today was colder. Up the long slope from Lake Michigan the wind tasted Mitchell Avenue, sorted through the gutters for small papers and grains of dust, and then set them down gently against the curbs.

Lon saw Hermine a block away, her small figure in a belted jacket leaning against the smoky brick of the building there. She was looking around at everything and nothing.

"Hold it, Renton," Demuth said, grinning. "We see her, so don't run. Running to meet a woman gives them the wrong idea. They get to believing they can drag us around."

"Sure," said Bo. "They can scheme plenty for a guy who's too eager."

While he talked, Kalinsky stretched his pale lips across a mouthful of big teeth. His thin, delicate nostrils were pale blue this morning in just a hint of frost. Anyone knew that his knowledge of girls was nothing at all and that he yearned to have a girl himself, any girl.

Lon hardly heard either one because he was straining ahead to see Hermine, who looked frail and sweet as a lost kitten surrounded by hostile elements. She had become the symbol of everything he thought was alive and decent. He took his moods from her, and once when they'd quarreled over nothing, he'd walked the streets for hours until he'd found her leaning against a wall like that one. He had asked her humbly to forgive him.

"Lon," she'd said in a small white voice, "am I ever glad you're here. I thought—I thought we'd lost each other."

When they reached her corner, Lon turned to his

74

friends. "See you around today," he said, lifting his hand in a gesture. They spoke briefly to Hermine and moved on.

She smiled up at him with her lips rosy and her eyes filled with wanton mischief.

"You may carry my books in the approved manner," she said. "I notice all the boys doing it for their girls. Here—"

She thrust one thin volume into his hands.

"I thought you said 'books.' This is a book. One book."

She laughed. "That's what I meant. You can carry my book."

He glanced at the title, which was something about Shakespeare. Hermine was always a surprise, and if she'd taken the book home, it meant that she had read it, because her high school record was full of top grades in everything from math to English.

Besides that, she read the daily newspaper. "It's because of Papa," she explained once to Lon. "He'll come to the breakfast table with the most solemn look, and pull in his mouth corners like this—" She did it. "Then he'll say, 'Do any of you here realize what those Red Chinese are doing?' "

"What do you do? Answer?"

"No," laughing, "I ask questions. I say, 'Did they set off another nuclear device, Papa, or have they crossed the border into—' "

"Does he answer them?"

"Of course," Hermine had said. "But he looks at me in such a funny way. 'Where did you hear about that? In school?' he'll say. 'No, Papa,' I'll tell him, 'not in school.' I don't think he even dreams that I open the paper every morning before he sees it and I glance over the headlines of the big stories. Then I roll it back up and put the rubber band around it again. That's mean of me, isn't it?"

"No," he'd told her, because it wasn't.

Mr. Mannheim was crazy about his youngest daughter, and the chances were he knew what the game was all along and liked to play it as well as she did.

Hermine's only school trouble was that sometimes she had an alarming honesty that could panic adults. For instance, if the dean of girls asked her why she wasn't getting along so well in a certain class, she was likely to tell exactly why—from a personality clash to subject matter.

She had a disconcerting way of taking for granted that he knew everything she did, which wasn't always so, especially with a girl who had strong opinions on nearly everything.

Yes, Hermine was different from any girl he'd ever known before. Right now, Lon tried the small book in his jacket pocket and found that it fit exactly. Then they set out for the high school blocks away.

They walked hand in hand for a while, in silence until Hermine took hers away, wet a finger in her mouth, and held it up.

"That's a north wind," she said with mock sagacity. "It'll be winter soon."

It was a safe prediction. "It's still warm," he scoffed, teasing. "Why talk about winter as if you can predict the weather? How do you know this isn't the year when it won't freeze at all? You'll have sunflowers growing all over town in January."

"Because I know," she said mysteriously. "Its going to be a very cold winter—"

"How can you be sure just by holding up one finger?"

"Easy," she shrugged. "Papa says so and he's never wrong—"

76

"I thought—"

"I mean about the weather. He tells weather by how the floor creaks in our house in certain places—"

"You're kidding—"

"No," she said solemnly to demonstrate her honest nature. "It's true. If the boards creak a lot in a certain way, it means a long, cold winter—"

It turned out that Hermine loved winter best, because she could go skating and in all this world there was nothing she liked better. To her, skating was like dancing, only infinitely more fun because it set a person that much more free. On ice skates she felt like a bird gliding down the wind, she said.

"You'll love it too, Lon," she told him. "Wait and see."

"Oh, sure," he said confidently. Wherever Hermine was would be the place for him, winter, autumn, night, or noon. He'd go there and like it.

Ahead of them was the high school, gray in the morning light, with storied room for a huge mass of kids. It wasn't like any school he'd known in California, although the teaching seemed about the same. A California high school usually was a complex of one-story buildings spread out all over and connected by walkways and a sweep of green lawn. This one was a machine standing right up to the street.

He didn't care. Hermine had shown him around and helped him with his program so that he fit in here as inconspicuously as possible. His classes were heavily academic and therefore boring to him, but he worked every day at the books to keep from being noticed by the teachers.

There was a sort of anonymous security here. In a small school, there were plenty of pressures on everyone to score. Here in this metropolitan high school most of that was gone. Sure, there were all the clubs, the athletic program, and special interest groups from dramatics to journalism and photography.

But nobody hounded a guy to choose any of them out of competition or needing to belong. If he wanted to stay on the outside of activities, it was all right with them. When he'd completed the state requirements he could go on to graduation or drop out, get a job, or join the services. They even had continuation school in the city.

Lon liked the arrangement that way because it kept school time to a bare minimum of a person's day. Hermine belonged to the Art Club, which met but seldom. Thus they sat in class six hours a day, listened to the teachers, and did the prescribed work. That way they earned a limited freedom where time became their own.

For the first time, Lon was able to keep adults in proper perspective. He was only a series of test records in a grade book, and they were impersonal human beings seen from a distance—although Miss Foelske, who taught English, and Mr. Lehrer, the math teacher, impressed him as being fairly interesting people.

Miss Foelske was tall, blond, and pretty. She read poetry to her classes as if it were something lovely she yearned to share, and her voice had a haunting feminine quality Lon liked.

Lehrer, on the other hand, was tough even to his appearance, which featured a jutting jaw shaved blue. But he made the material understandable and stuck with it until everyone knew the terms. If Lon got to know a teacher here, it would be one of those, but of course that would never happen.

He lived each day for the last bell. Then he would meet

Hermine near the main entrance and they would walk home together the long way around, idling down Mitchell and staring into shop windows, or sitting on a bench somewhere—anything in which they were together.

That afternoon, Hermine said, "Do you know what homemaking is, Lon?"

It was a required course she had postponed to her senior year because Miss Gertrude Warneke taught it, but that wasn't the right answer.

"No," he said. "I don't."

"Guess."

"I can't. How would I know anything about homemaking?"

"You might if you tried, but I knew you wouldn't," Hermine said triumphantly, lifting her chin and pointing it around like a bird waggling a beak. "Miss Warneke says it's a woman's personality brought to bear in the home—The community, if not the nation, depends on—" She glanced at him hard. "Are you listening to me, Lon Renton? Homemaking is—Do you know what we had today?"

"Naturally not."

"Glassware—" Hermine said like a truth revealed. "There is more to glassware than an ordinary peasant like you might think, Lon, my boy. Properly arranged, glassware can do wonders, lending grace and distinction, not to mention dignity, to any table. But we must always remember this about glassware—"

"Go on," he said, "—what do we have to remember about—"

"Homemaking," Hermine whispered, moistening her lips first. "Uh—tell me you love me, Lon."

"Naturally," he said.

"Say it."

"I love you," he told her.

Her eyes widened in grievous outrage. "Not that way," she complained, "as if we'd been married for ten years. Say it—say it with feeling. No"—glancing around—"not right now. Wait until those people—"

He did. Then, "I love you," he repeated, with feeling.

"More feeling, please. Pretend we're sitting at this table surrounded by all this gracious glassware, and—and candles in silver sticks, and—"

He had to laugh at her because she could get so silly.

"Come on," he said, taking her hand. "Let's go home."

That's what they did—went home to Hermine's house. Mrs. Mannheim welcomed Lon with her eyes growing almost as soft as her daughter's. She always brought him coffee and cookies if he wanted them, or a glass of milk.

She was a great believer in the powers of milk to heal whatever was wrong with youth, and one of her regrets was that Hermine detested the stuff.

"I can't understand why," Mrs. Mannheim would say to Lon. "Both of her sisters, Hilda and Eva, loved milk. And look at her: scrawny and pinched, as if—Oh, I don't know—"

"You see," Hermine would call upon Lon, seeking justice. "You notice how my mother calls me names. Scrawny. Now tell the truth, Lon, am I scrawny or am I not fat the way Mamma is?" Her eyes would sparkle as she pinioned him in that kind of dilemma.

Mrs. Mannheim never permitted him to answer.

"Oh, all right, Hermine," she'd say. "You can eat cookies and drink coffee. But leave Lon be. Let him drink his milk. You're a bad influence on all of us, contradicting your mother and saying she's fat when I only want you to drink a little milk and grow—"

"Ugh!" Hermine would respond, making a horrible face. "Poison from mulch cows. Baby food. It kills people, probably."

"What can I do?" Mrs. Mannheim would implore, shrugging and taking things from the table. "What can anyone do with such a willful, headstrong daughter? Nothing."

Afterward, Hermine and Lon usually did homework at the kitchen table, separately, but helping each other if they could until the afternoon sun grew into long shadows and the dinner hour was near.

Lon stayed often, uneasy in Mr. Mannheim's silence, but not enough to refuse. At first he always called Thelma to say he'd be late, but finally he stopped bothering to do that.

The home against which Hermine rebelled in her way was something else to Lon. Even with Mr. Mannheim's austere and bleak manner there was none of the unexpected and a person knew where he stood. The truth was that for the first time Lon felt secure, with a new relationship to the present time and the future. He felt the stirrings within him of a hidden man who needed to emerge and go somewhere, do these things.

Hermine sensed it too. Sometimes she would put her hand on his arm. "Lon," she'd say in a voice unlike her usual calm, "what are we going to do—"

"Do? About what—"

"About us. About next year when—"

"Oh, that—" he'd reply in a strong tone. "Easy. Ask me something hard, why don't you?"

"Is it easy, Lon?" she'd whisper. "I mean, really—"

"Sure. We'll get married, that's all. How hard is it to get married?" snapping fingers. "Hah—why, people do it all the time. Everybody gets married—"

"But—but, Lon," Hermine would say, clinging to his arm in that possessive style, "it isn't that easy for us. You've—you've got to go on to school, like your brothers, you said, and—"

"Maybe," he would say. "Let's wait and see, Hermine."

6

THE LAWNS TURNED brown and the last leaves fell from the trees until their branches became the bare veins of a leaden sky. Rain fell often, with heavy, irritable lightning muttering across the city, icing the streets and sometimes piling dirty slush in gutters.

Thelma was teaching again. With only a couple of years to go before compulsory retirement, she acted as if there was something at the school she couldn't afford to miss no matter how weary she was of the routine. She was out of the house before Lon left for high school and often stayed late for teachers meetings.

She worried because she wasn't home more and blamed herself for Lon's increasing tendency to stay away. Once when his father was bawling him out for coming in so late, she'd interceded.

"There's nothing very cheerful for him to come home to, Harold," she'd insisted. "When his school is over, I'm not home and you're out until all hours. He doesn't want to be alone in this big house. Naturally he'd much rather talk with—with his friends."

"Why doesn't he have his friends come here?" Harold Renton wanted to know.

"He's perfectly welcome to. You are, you know, Lon. But—"

Her voice trailed off and she'd stared out of the window as if she heard the voices of a multitude of welcome young people in times past.

Thelma had told Lon of those days when this place was supposed to have rocked with laughter and good times. Carlos and Robbie were at home, and they made the difference, she said.

They farmed celery as a cash crop out on the western edge of town. Carlos was a big, ruined hulk who needed to talk loudly to feel important, Lon guessed. He'd been a rookie pitcher for the White Sox when he was young, signing the contract right from high school and fizzling out in the minors before people even knew he'd left town. Evidently he'd never caught on that he wasn't still a young sport or whatever they called them in his day. He drove around town in an open convertible no matter what the weather, and he had a bull whip in the car with which he practiced all the time he wasn't doing something else. He was pretty good at snapping the heads of dandelions or obliterating a cigarette laid down as a target, but what good was that?

Robbie was a smaller man who was still fighting the War where he'd made it to captain. He and the men, as he called them, had been on the beach at Anzio and that experience had done something permanent to Robbie because even Thelma called him "The Captain" a lot of the time. He had the farmhouse decorated with his war relics, medals, pistols including Lugers, bayonets, defused grenades, and some Nazi banners. He smoked cigarettes constantly, letting them hang crumpled from his lips so that they wiggled while he talked, and all the time his pale-blue eyes, held unblinking, would shift around as though looking for something.

Robbie had been married for a time, but something had happened to his wife which was connected with the war, too, as if she were a battle casualty and nobody ever talked about her. Carlos, like Thelma, had remained single.

"He couldn't have settled down," she said of him. "He was too restless and high-spirited for a calm little life."

Since their father had died, Thelma had this house and "the boys," as she called them, got the farm. They had managed the place, hiring out the heavy work and selling off acreage in bad years. Occasionally they ran the tractors around to show visitors how they were keeping a hand in the work.

It was a terrible judgment for anyone Lon's age to get to thinking of his stepuncles as "boys" too, but the alternative was to regard them for what they really were—a couple of big, lazy slobs, and they didn't quite qualify there.

In fact, they'd treated Lon decently whenever he went out to the farm, stopping what they were doing long enough to welcome him. And when they visited Thelma, they did one act that Lon always admired; they turned up the thermostat.

"Will you look at this?" Carlos would bellow, checking the instrument. "She wants us to freeze, men. Why, Sis, it's only fifty-four in here. What do you think we are, polar bears?"

Then they'd run the indicator up to eighty or ninety and allow a little warm air to flow in through the radiators from the oil burner below. The coal furnace had been converted last year.

Either Thelma had nutty ideas about health, which could be true, or she didn't understand thermostats. Whatever the reason, she never moved the indicator above sixty and neither did his father—although Lon noticed him bringing in wood and building a fire as often as possible.

Hot or cold, the house didn't bother Lon, especially upstairs in his room, where he figured the heat could never go anyway. He'd solved that problem by cultivating lightning speed in getting dressed, shaved, and out. Once out, he stayed out unless he planned to go to bed.

Inevitably, there were some afternoons when he was alone in the big house. There were no locked doors and he had the full run of it from attic to basement if he cared.

He had never gone beyond the doorsill of the room next to his, but he'd glanced inside once or twice. It was a huge bedroom with a black marble corner fireplace and ceiling-length wine red draperies. The four-poster bed was high and dainty with a ruffled cover, plump pillows with lace, and the air of recent occupancy with the dresser covered with a woman's personal gear—combs, brushes, and a mirror backed with tarnished and curled gold. An ornate glass-enclosed clock stood on the mantel, where pieces of iridescent glassware were arranged beside it.

Here Thelma's mother had died and the hands of the clock were supposed to be set at the exact moment, with the things on the dresser in the identical places they had been on that tragic night. Or so Thelma believed, although

Lon couldn't see it because she dusted and cleaned here once a week and shoved everything around to do the job.

"Don't ever go in there, Lon," his father had cautioned him in private. "I don't. Your stepmother is sensitive about the way things are placed, and if you broke something, or—"

Lon had nodded, ashamed that his dad had thought it necessary to tell him. Perhaps that was why he did go into their room—the master bedroom at the stair landing—one afternoon. It was directly above the music room, and he was actually only curious to see how the bay window treatment was carried into the second floor.

In the alcove Thelma had a dressing table with a wide mirror that showed deterioration and yellowing around the edges. Her things were similar to her mother's except that the mirror and combs were backed with silver instead of gold.

Elsewhere there was a desk, spindly chairs with fringes and fluting, but the twin beds were maple and seemed more modern. Lon was about to leave when the desk caught his eye. A book was lying open there and his glance was drawn to it irresistibly. He ran through a couple of lines of print; then turned to the title, keeping his finger in the place. *The Adolescent Boy* it read; something like that.

He replaced the book precisely so and glanced coldly at the others set between wrought iron bookends: *Leaves of Grass, The Long Valley,* and a couple of thin volumes of poetry by Edna St. Vincent Millay. But it was the others that Lon saw with narrow eyes: *The Years Between, Angry Children, Our Disturbed Youth*—stuff like that.

Lon stared at them while he comprehended the meaning of their existence. Then he went out quickly and tried not to think of Thelma and his father, but when they kept crowding back into his mind, he telephoned Hermine and talked with her for an hour.

At last when his stepmother returned, he greeted her with the cool and classic manner of the teen-age rebel.

"Lon," she sang out, "how nice to have you home. How was school today?"

"All right."

She accepted that. The books had probably told her to accept anything from the poor sick little kid. She carried a grocery sack, which she set down on the dining room table.

He strolled over and stared into her eyes, through them. "I'll put this in the kitchen," he said. "Anything more in the car—"

"No-o," she said uncertainly. "That's all."

She stood there stripping her brown gloves from bony fingers. Her coat and umbrella that she always carried in fall weather had been put away in the entry hall according to her habit.

He returned from the kitchen and sank again into the chair where he had been sitting.

"Lon—"

"Yes," turning slowly.

"How do you like it here—I mean, by now—Here in Milwaukee. Do you like the high school?"

"Fine," he said in a dead, flat voice, smiling a flat smile. Then let her mind flip through the book pages for the answer to that one. She probably wanted a lot more: that his classes were interesting, the school charming, and that he'd made a host of bully buddies.

She had a little trick of shaking her head involuntarily when she was nervous or very tired, and she did that now —so hard that a strand of her iron-gray hair shook loose in front and dangled toward her eyebrow. It gave her fierce neatness an unexpectedly frowsy appearance.

"Lon—" she said, making a little gesture down at her side with her left hand and stepping toward him, "I've been thinking a good deal lately about—well, about us."

"Us?" he asked in that contemptuous, maddening voice so many kids used, guaranteed to raise the blood pressure of any adult. "You and I?"

It didn't work that way with Thelma. She laughed. "Yes, you and I—although as a teacher I suppose I should tell you that it really should be 'you and me.' Only an English teacher or a mother has a right to correct a person's grammar, I'm told, and I'm not either of those. Yes, you and I—but actually the three of us together. The—the family—"

Despite those books upstairs, Lon had to admit to himself that it was hard to keep the mood with Thelma. His manner softened.

"I—" he began, "I suppose you want us to be happy together and—well, all that, don't you?" In a way, he meant it as a compliment.

"Not exactly, Lon," she replied, growing serious. "I doubt that I have the ability to make people happy. But what I'm striving for is somewhat close to happiness, I think. I'd—" She glanced out through the window toward the street where the sky had grown wintery at this time of afternoon. "I'd wish us to understand each other first of all, and then to—well, to like each other—"

She waited while a silence grew in the room to make the clock on the wall important.

89

Books or not, the idea caught Lon. Most adults hollered around about how much they loved. But not Thelma; she was willing to settle for something human and reasonable.

"Why not?" he finally said. "It's a good idea."

She had sat down in the chair near him and gotten out a little handkerchief from somewhere which she was twisting in her thin hands now hidden in her lap.

"You see, Lon," she said as strongly as she could, "I haven't any real experience with—with boys your age. I don't know whether I'm doing things right because —the generations change, you know. I can't even look into my own girlhood and discover much that applies to you and your friends, except perhaps some very basic things—"

"You're doing fine," he said with too much purpose. "We—we dig each other, to use the corny expression."

You couldn't talk to Thelma that way.

"It's nice of you to say so," she replied, "but I'm afraid it isn't true. I think we have a long way to go, Lon, even if we both try hard—"

Her raw honesty shook him; he admired her as a just and reasonable adult, one of the few he'd met in life. That was what had nailed him about the books; she should have played it freehand, and cool.

Now, right this minute, he wanted to be as honest as she was—to tell her the blunt truth: that in this phase he probably couldn't understand any adult, let alone his stepmother; that his mother's death and the loneliness of Greyrock had done something to him that he needed to think through in his own way and his own time. Then, later on, he would understand and when he had the words to say so he'd tell them in a hundred ways—that he was grateful, and had loved them all along.

Yet he didn't say that. The truth was too stern for a teen-ager to tell any of them until they had perceived it themselves.

Sure enough, she beat him to the punch. "It isn't quite fair for me to speak so bluntly about understanding. We think it should come to us naturally, but it doesn't. Sometimes it takes years"—her expression became almost wistful—and we have to wait. But that's the way I am, Lon. I'm trying to cut corners. To hurry."

"Doesn't everybody?" Lon asked, hearing his patronizing tone without satisfaction. "It's human—"

Thelma stood up. "No, I disagree with you. Not everyone does. A lot of people learn to be patient." She smiled again. "What I'm saying, Lon, is that I like nearly everything I know about you. I hope you'll like me as much." She made an open gesture with both of her skinny arms and laughed wryly. "Nobody wants to be a cruel stepmother, Lon, no matter how many of us really are. We stepmothers are a little jealous, perhaps, and we want a—a better image, I think they call it nowadays—"

Her laughter got to him. "You'll never make it!" he said.

"Make what?"

"Make it to cruel stepmother."

"Just to plain stepmother, Lon?"

So here it was again—the moment and the opportunity that she had offered a hundred times. But the books upstairs got in the way; this cold house; the statue in the alcove—

"Yes," he said. "I—"

"That's good enough for me," Thelma interrupted, marching back to the dining room, "and it's the nicest thing anyone has said all day. Well, I must get busy. Your father will want his dinner soon."

She did that, and for a while Lon sat unmoved in the chair while she rattled the pans in the kitchen. After a while, he went upstairs to his room, going the long way around. He felt like an idiot.

Later on they had dinner together, the three of them, in the dining room for a change. Lon sat opposite Thelma, who served and removed the plates with long strides back and forth to the kitchen.

"School's going all right?" his father asked in that way of parents who have forgotten all about the way a school goes.

"Sure, Dad," Lon replied, focusing his eyes on Harold Renton's hands. His father's once strong hands seemed now like limp white birds, flapping a way home as he gestured.

"Good," said Mr. Renton. "Glad you've gotten the hang of it."

"Another bowl of this nice soup, Lon?" Thelma asked, holding a silver tureen and the ladle.

"No, thank you," he said.

"Of course he wants more soup," said his father. "Go ahead and give him some more. Wonderful dinner tonight." He kept watching the ladle. "No, give it to the boy, my dear. It's good for him. Somebody has to—"

"Lon?" Thelma asked, the ladle still poised.

"I'd rather not," he said, "because a guy—" He was going to tell her that a person could hold only so much celery in any one given day. But he didn't.

She set the tureen down carefully and covered it. That ended the matter except for a moment of heavy silence within which Lon felt his father's stare and saw his gray, shaggy eyebrows drawn down.

Nothing more was said. The meal continued. For dessert there was some gelatin with fruit scattered through its pink tissues. Thelma had made it the night before and it wasn't bad.

Lon finished his portion in continued silence until he excused himself and left the table, glad to get away.

He wasn't alone for long. While Thelma clattered the dishes, Lon heard his father moving behind him.

"Lon!"

"Yes, sir," turning slowly.

"I'd like to talk with you."

He shrugged faintly. Adults began that way so often he'd come to know the sentence as a threat.

"All right."

"We can go out there," pointing toward the music room and leading the way.

Lon waited while the older man fumbled for the switch on the fussy lamp. The bits of colored glass cast a curiously comic light over the scene, something as pink as the gelatin and like it.

"That bowl of soup—" Harold Renton began—

Some force stirred within Lon. Justice. "Dad," he said with a grave, pleading voice, "you know that a person can absorb only so much celery, so why—"

"Because I say so," said his father. "Thelma wished you to have it and you refused!"

"Sure. Why not?" Lon asked with genuine curiosity. "If I didn't want more celery soup, why did I have to choke it down?"

"Don't be impertinent, young man," said Mr. Renton, coloring in the strange light but holding his voice with heavy control, "don't you comprehend that your stepmother is trying to help you? To be—to fill an empty place in your life?"

"Yes—" truthfully, "but that doesn't mean she has to stuff me with celery sou—"

"Be more civil," his father snapped. "And kinder. The next time she offers you something extra, take it and be glad you have it. Why must you confuse insolence with independence?"

A responding anger flooded through Lon and tingled in his face. He was neither of those—insolent or independent. Not yet. The hot words pushed against his throat. He wanted to yell at his father about how wrong he was to bring his phony idea of discipline into this scene—to lay down the law about a stupid bowl of soup—But when he met Harold Renton's eyes he knew it was useless to say anything at all.

"I don't know why," he mumbled instead.

The old man tried to vest his words with profound judgment and unforgettable truth. "It's not just a bowl of soup, Lon. I've talked with you about helping us before, and now I'll say it again. I won't have you crossing your stepmother that way—ever. I want you to do what she says no matter what that may be. Do you understand?"

Lon looked away. "Yes," he said in a dull voice. He did; much too well.

Harold Renton let the message sink in for a moment. "Very well," he finished. "I'll accept that. Now let's go back to the living room and behave like gentlemen."

"Gentlemen?" Lon echoed. "That's how?"

"Certainly. March on in there."

Lon did, and there ended the last chance he had to become Thelma's friend. As soon as he could he escaped upstairs to his cold and dreary room and sat alone in the darkness.

7

WINTER IN Wisconsin was a real shock to Lon. It screamed in one evening on a north wind that bit into the city with hurting needles of cold. Then sleet came, driving vertically into all the pockets of human warmth.

All night long the storm moaned around Thelma's old house like a thing alive and suffering. It wakened Lon a dozen times; he would lie still, listening and wondering why people chose to live in a place like this. Finally he fell into deep sleep and when he roused in the morning the world was too still and silent to be real.

His window had frosted closed, inside and out, and it wasn't until he had gone downstairs, shivering, that he saw what winter could do. The heavy fall of snow had transmuted all the dark and dirty places in the neighborhood into a luminescent veil of white crystal upon which sunlight glistened and struck out sparks of dazzle.

But what Lon saw most were the icicles hung like glass fangs along the eaves and on every overhanging surface. The snow had melted there from residual heat after the winds stopped and created the frigid points that captured light and twisted it painfully.

Lon knew by instinct that he wouldn't like such a winter. In California, a person went up to Yosemite, or Big Bear for the sports. He dressed for the trip, usually on a weekend, and when it was over he came back into his expected world that was green and flowery. Nobody in California really had a home in the snow. Winter was a Christmas tree decoration.

Thelma was in the kitchen watching him, but he didn't notice her until she spoke.

"Isn't it beautiful, Lon?" she asked with all her enthusiasm. "Isn't it perfectly beautiful? I just love the first real snow best of the whole winter."

"Beautiful?" he said, testing the word and staring out again.

"Oh, yes," Thelma cried. "Lovely, perfectly lovely—" She stalked toward him with so much vigor that it made her skirt swirl and her gray hair fluff. "You'll think so too, Lon, as soon as you're out there and see what it's done to the whole city. It makes everything seem new, and—and like a gift."

"It is beautiful," he admitted slowly. A few things were: Hermine—the snow—a field of California lupine—

"Yes, and—" She suddenly looked him over very thoughtfully. "So many things to do—" she mused. "Why, you have only that wool jacket, Lon, and—Why, we should have bought your overcoat long ago. I noticed some yesterday in Sweinert's window as I drove by, but it didn't register that—I must be growing more forgetful—" She seemed downright sorry.

"It's all right—" he said.

"No. No, it isn't. You need a coat immediately. And gloves. You'll need heavy, lined gloves and some galoshes

—And"—growing arch—"could you abide winter underwear if I picked up some?" She laughed now. "They call them 'thermal' lately, but I don't have a speck of pride about wearing longies in cold weather. Of course, I'm an old lady—"

Lon was embarrassed. The list of clothing shocked him because he had told himself fiercely that at least they wouldn't need to buy him anything. The uniforms at Greyrock had kept his suit practically new and everything was still in style. The stuff she'd mentioned would cost plenty and he'd have to show appreciation for a year.

"Whatever you say," he ventured, "but I really don't need a thing. This jacket—" demonstrating its thickness, "keeps me hot. And—well, I really don't like a lot of things to lose—galoshes and gloves—"

"Tush!" she said, as if to make a joke of the expense. "You don't know Milwaukee winters, Lon. It gets truly cold here, and you even should have a hat. I realize that not a soul in California wears a hat—the men, I mean—but here they do."

"A hat?" He grinned at that picture. "Hey, are you serious?"

"I should say I am," she replied. "Any—"

He stopped and turned toward the doorway, where Harold Renton had appeared, looking gray beneath his skin.

"Dear," she said, "do you know what we've done?"

"No," he said dully, perhaps expecting the worst.

"We've completely forgotten our boy. He doesn't have any winter clothing; none at all. He'll be soaking wet by the time he gets to school this morning. The snow looks fine, but I can tell it's soft and the sidewalks will be—"

"Don't you have an overcoat?" Lon's father asked reproachfully, as if he might have had one of fine cashmere and thrown it away one night on a whim. "What happened to—"

"He has only that jacket, Harold, and a rather nice suit. But his underwear—" She shook her head. "Thin cotton and not much of that."

"No overcoat," said his father in a flat tone. "Probably no gloves, and—Those things will cost a good deal, Thelma. He might need to wait—for a few days—"

"Of course not!" she declared. "He must go to—let me see—Gimbels? Yes, I still have an account there. Lon, this very afternoon as soon as school is over you take the bus all the way downtown. Go to Gimbels and get yourself a coat of substantial quality—a winter coat, mind you. And don't forget galoshes, gloves, and a scarf." She smiled. "I'll allow you to decide for yourself about a hat and long underwear. Put the things on my account; you only need say, 'Charge this to Thelma Potter.' The account is under my old name."

The matter was settled because they finished breakfast without further mention of clothes. He thought they'd forgotten it and he wouldn't need to go to Gimbels and accept their charity.

But he was wrong. Thelma scraped the dishes quickly. She gave the impression of being some tall, unbelievable bird, but when she went upstairs afterward and came down dressed, her winter clothes gave her a buttoned and muffled appearance that was formidable.

"Now, Lon," she said sharply in the manner of adults who do good and know it, "don't you dare forget. Gimbels

98

this afternoon and no excuses. It's bad enough that you have to trudge all that distance even once. Don't you want to ride with me? If you hurry, I could run you to the high school and you'd have dry feet—"

"Thanks," he mumbled. "I'm afraid it'll take me too long to get ready." Thelma didn't know that he met Hermine every morning.

"Very well," she said, pursing her lips like a despairing mother over a six-year-old's antics. She shook her head ruefully. "Last winter I had the same trouble with your father, so don't think you're the only stubborn Californian in Milwaukee. I'm sure you need at least one day in wet snow, Lon, or you never would believe me. Isn't that true, Harold, dear?" She permitted her smile to become almost tender. "I noticed you got right into your longies this morning without a bit of protest."

It was an intimacy about Thelma and his dad that Lon would have preferred not to hear. He glanced at the man and neither spoke.

Thelma, always sensitive to emotional change, caught up the thread before it spun loose. "I really must run along," she said, switching subjects. "You don't suppose my radiator—Harold, we have antifreeze, don't we?"

"Yes," said Mr. Renton. "Besides, both cars are in the garage. They'll start."

"I know," Thelma returned. "That old car of mine is so reliable. Well, I must go. Are you coming, dear?"

Lon gave his father a sidelong glance. He was bundled into a huge brown coat and now he held a hat. The man followed along after Thelma and closed the vestibule door. The two of them made a scraping sound as they got into galoshes. Then the outer door closed.

But Lon could still hear Thelma's voice, brilliant with

clarity across the snow. "Oh, it's perfectly magnificent—" she sang out for all the world and the neighbors to hear. "Utterly breathtaking, isn't it, Harold?"

What Lon's father thought of the snowfall, good or ill, was said so quietly that nobody heard. But if he claimed it was anything but terrible, it had to be a lie because winter was already in his father's bones with a desperate cold.

For an instant he felt sorry for them both. Age seemed a condition that happened to others and would never come to him no matter how hard he tried to understand its riddle of how it changed people. Yet Thelma seemed to be permanently of her age and time, as if she had been born this way. But he could feel no genuine empathy for either one; they both belonged somewhere else and in another time.

The telephone rang.

It was Hermine with her voice skipping down the wire and entering his blood through fingertips.

"Lon," she chattered way out, forming an image of snow sprites and glass reindeer, "isn't this snow something? I mean, did you dream that it happened this way—overnight?"

She meant the ice and sleet too. Human beings around here all seemed to welcome the chance to freeze to death.

"What is?" he came back, teasing her. "You mean this little dab of snow out there, Hermine?"

"Yes," she screeched. "All that glorious white lace. Also ice. Ice is very German, Lon. It rates high in the best circles." She paused and took a deep breath. "Little dab?" remembering. "Why, it's a full ten inches, the paper said. Papa had to shovel the whole walk to find it—"

"To find it?"

There was silence.

"Hermine—" he said.

More silence.

"Hermine, are you there?"

"Of course I'm here," she said testily. "It was to find the Milwaukee *Journal*, Lon. Don't you like the snow?" She acted as if she were a hostess concerned over the behavior of an irascible guest.

"Sure," he told her. "I like it. It's great, I guess. I was only kidding you a little. You see, in California we go up to the snow and the drifts are ten feet deep, powdery dry, and the sun is warm."

"That's up in the mountains," she said, "the Sierras, you told me. When you've had enough fun you drive home through these miles and miles of orange blossoms, Shasta daisies, and—"

"Not exactly," he admitted lamely. "That's an exaggeration, but—"

"Do you really know how to ice-skate, Lon?" she asked suddenly. "You said you did, you know."

He'd been on skates a couple of times and didn't remember much about it because the occasions were a long time ago. "Sure," he told her. "Why?"

"Wondering. Well, I've got to start soon if I'm going to meet you."

"Here, too—" He glanced at his drugstore watch. "But fast. Hang up, Hermine. Right now."

She did but not before making a kissing sound into the receiver that was so close and personal he could almost feel it on his lips. "Thanks," he said in a low tone. "I needed that, and I love you."

In his imagination he could hear her feet scampering around while she gave her mixed-up banter with her mother before she slammed the door and hit the porch. He savored the image for a moment and then left the house and stepped outside into winter.

As usual, he picked up Demuth, Kalinsky, and Jerzy Starkiewicz, whom everyone called Starky. He wore glasses and had his hair combed straight forward in a style that made him look like a total moron.

Actually, Starkiewicz was the brain of the crowd, a senior and straight "A" student with an inborn understanding of math that could scare ordinary people.

When he was about three, Jerzy had run around the dirty sidewalks chanting singsong with algebra for lyrics. Now the entire Starkiewicz family, iron workers mostly, expected him to get in there, make good grades in college, work for the government or industry, and lift them out of the black hole previous generations of them had dug.

It drove them wild that Starky hung around with the Greenfields, playing games and in between helping to look for trouble down at the pool hall. They lectured him every day about it, and he'd stand there saying, "All right. All right. I won't do it anymore."

Then he'd go out and do anything he pleased with unmatched coolness.

He had a wispy girl named Lidia, with long sorrel-blond hair and huge eyes. She could think up more wrong deeds for Jerzy to pull than anyone else.

"She's got my old man half insane all the time," Starkiewicz would say in his husky, scholarly voice. "'Get rid of that girl,' he'll holler like a big troll."

"What's a troll?" Kalinsky would ask. "You told me once, Starky. I think you said it was Norwegian for 'monster,' but I've forgotten."

"It's something that acts like my old man," Jerzy might tell him. Sometimes Jerzy had a mean streak in him, as if he were laughing at the other guys from his high brain position. Colleges were already inquiring about him because he went off the board in their tests.

He hated his whole family for not letting him be human, he sometimes complained.

"They act as if I were a freak," he'd once told Lon. "I'm this valuable rotten egg they want to sell to the highest bidder."

He'd glanced at Lon, with his face a portrait of self-pity.

"I sometimes want a real father and mother. I even used to feel like crying about it, but now I feel like hitting something hard. So once I cut my father's old-fashion razor strop almost in half and I blamed it on one of my brothers, the oldest one. When the old man caught on, he wanted to whip me with the long end of the strop, but my mother kept hollering, 'Stephan! Stephan! Stop! You'll hurt his brains.' My father kept saying he couldn't hurt brains from that end of me, but she made him stop anyway. My lovely brains are money to my mother, she thinks. She says, 'My boy Jerzy will keep me in my age.' Now, is that a mother?"

"I don't know," Lon had replied truthfully. What did he know about mothers?

Later on, he was going to wonder if what happened began with Starky's talk about his family.

"You know, Renton," he volunteered one afternoon, "I'll be the first person in my family to finish high school."

He said it out of context, as if his thinking ran along by itself without reference to other people around him. The Greenfields had been considering going down to Kosciusko Park to pick up the action there.

"It's true," Jerzy had gone on. "They all quit and went to work earning money: my brothers, my father, my uncles —everyone. Why, I can remember how it was with Steve, my middle brother. He wanted to graduate because the counselor, or maybe it was the coach, had begun talking to him about college—" Jerzy had laughed and showed his rotten front teeth. "Know what my old man said?"

"No."

"He said, 'You want to be educated, Steve? You want to learn more than your father, I see. A smart, education fool, huh? Well let me tell you I left school after six, seven years and I done all right. I put food on this table every day, and this roof I kept up with seven lousy kids and paid the mortgage. Now you gonna read a slide rule and do like the counselor said, go up to Ripon College or something? You gonna be a teacher, maybe, and teach the old man his lessons, hah?' "

There was a silence.

"What happened?" Lon had asked.

Starky gave a round-shouldered shrug. "What could happen, Renton? Nothing. You were telling me how your brothers went to college so that ups your chances and mine stay the same. I read some facts from the State of Maryland—a survey. Know what they found? Nearly all the kids who drop out of high school have parents who dropped out too. So they drum into a guy's head from babyhood up that school is really useless and education makes people foolish. In his last year, the dropout proves he's no good; he doesn't do any work and just stares out

104

the window. So they flunk him out, and then he can say, 'See! My father was right.'"

"Well?"

"Well this, Renton: the only reason they don't do me like my brother Steve is that I'm worth money. I'm marketable, the way Miss Neuhauser keeps saying in social studies. I get to like school because nobody else in my family did. You don't like school because your brothers graduated and went to college and now your father is too broke to send you. So where's the sense?"

There wasn't any. Jerzy's mother made him stay in every day for a couple of hours' study when he didn't need to crack a book. He was a genius, probably, right up on the math and science wave crest of the future.

Playing football, Starky would suddenly laugh after he'd been tackled or something. "Don't hurt his hands," he'd holler. "That's what my mother says. 'Don't hit him on the knuckles, Stephan.' Somebody told her you needed hands to work a slide rule."

Right now as soon as he'd hit the street, Lon realized that Thelma knew what she was talking about. By the time he'd joined his buddies the cold had gouged through the soft leather of his oxfords and stung his feet into numbness, wet and freezing. Halfway to the corner where he always met Hermine, the wind coming up from ice-plated Lake Michigan rammed frosty tongues through his light jacket. It was ten times, a hundred times, colder this morning than yesterday. His soaked feet flamed in fiery cold and within the jacket he shivered while little droplets of his breath froze on the lapels and melted away.

Even Jerzy wore an overcoat of sorts, his being dark blue and polished at the elbows, bigger than the guy inside its capacious folds. Bo and Demuth had coats of good

105

heavy stuff, woolen scarves, and galoshes, with Kalinsky in earmuffs alone but the rest wearing hats and gloves.

Significantly, it was Starky who noticed Lon's lack of winter gear. "Man," he said, "where's your stuff? Your coat, and—" He fell abruptly silent.

"Yeah," Kalinsky offered. "Maybe not this morning, but some mornings around here a guy in your shape could freeze his ears. Nose, too. Also fingers—" Bo thrust out his hands, stuffed in thick woolen mittens.

"Knew this goof who froze his ears," Dick Demuth said into the gap of his overcoat. "A guy looks peculiar without ears. It's the only real use I ever heard for them."

"What is?" Bo demanded.

"To keep you from looking peculiar—on each side of your head, naturally," Dick said, pouring laughter into his coat like steam. "Kalinsky, sometimes you're stupid."

Jerzy said, "No, he isn't Dick. Kalinsky is smart. He keeps his mouth shut in school and gets decent grades. Teachers even like him. It's you who's stupid, Demuth. You wise off all the time when this crazy world isn't one bit funny. There's nothing funny about a person's ears falling off, know that."

Demuth hesitated. "I know a joke that'll make you laugh, Starky. Either you laugh or I give you a dollar. On?"

"No," said Jerzy. "I don't have a dollar."

Lon didn't see Hermine at their special corner. Not this morning. He was too busy stamping his feet to get back some circulation. His toes felt as if they'd frozen off and were rattling around inside his stony shoes. Probably his ears were next, and even his fingers seemed to chatter although they were stuffed into his jacket pockets, fists doubled and the fabric held close.

106

Down the arch of his face he could see his nose turned a kind of angry blue and getting worse. The early sunlight had disappeared. In its place was a ponderous, leaden atmosphere that bore in upon a person like a vast burden with no tangible weight of its own; nothing but an enveloping presence of penetrating cold.

Hermine was there, swathed in a bundle of woolly things —a scarf with bright yarn balls dangling, mittens, a deep, soft coat, boots, and high wool socks turned down cutely.

"See you, Renton," Jerzy said, forging on with Bo and Demuth, but glancing back for an instant as if he yearned for something left behind.

"By!" Hermine waved at them. "Don't study too hard before I get there, Jerzy."

Then she noticed Lon.

"Why—" she said, "why, you're not—" Her eyes narrowed and her mouth hardened. "Lon," she managed, "did Miss Potter—I mean, did your stepmother let you go out to walk a couple of miles in your summer slacks and tennis jacket?"

He didn't answer. For one reason, there wasn't time because Hermine hurried him to school as fast as she could scamper, sort of buzzing the whole time with vengeance for the forces of darkness that had let him out in the blizzard.

Inside the school, she marched him directly to the warmest place in the hall and stood with him there while he thawed.

By now he'd explained that a person who came from California isn't necessarily prepared for a bad day in Siberia. Thelma was blameless, he assured that girl. Both she and his father had far too much on their minds to care for every detail in the life of a seventeen-year-old

107

son. He had himself put off buying the stuff, but today he would take care of that little chore. And really, Hermine—

"It doesn't amount to a thing," he finished.

"Oh, naturally not," she said, "it's just silly of me, and downright German and meddlesome." She stared him right in the eye, closing one of hers. "Well, it just happens that I love you. I happen to need you for myself for always. I need your toes, ears, fingers—everything. And all without the taint of pneumonia. It's simple, and if you think about it a while it'll come to you."

"All right," he said. "Think. Think."

Nearby the river of high school ran, and outside the gray sky pushed downward into the streets. They greeted some people; it was surprising to Lon how many they knew.

Then, "Do you really know how to ice-skate?" Hermine asked.

"No," he said, trying truth for a change. "Not really."

She nodded. "I didn't think so. Well, I'll just have to teach you," finished Hermine resolutely.

8

ICE-SKATING? Take a pair of Swensen racing skates with the long and glittering hollow-ground blades and strap them to the feet of a fair-sized guy with glowering brows. Let him pull the laces up tight and snug around the tucked wool socks. Then walk him to the hard surface of Greenfield Pond that glared back the sky in mirror perfection this morning, but tonight is a white scuff from a million blade cuts.

Why, any young person could skate who's well past seventeen, coordinated into dexterity and grace, and who's not afraid he'll get hurt in the action and doesn't care too much if he is.

Ice-skate? Look, this youth-type out of the Golden State, where showers of flowers bloom in the sun, can do anything anyone else can do; he can play any sport.

The ski jump could be a little more complicated, naturally. Getting airborne didn't look so difficult, but hitting the slope at the right angle might require genuine know-how to keep from fracturing an arm or busting a skull.

It was something to remember, that first evening on the pond, partly because of Hermine's attitude toward skating, but far more because Lon finally realized that his decision had begun there, although it was weeks before he knew about it himself. There was nothing solid, of course, no irreversible words to pound home the message. The attitude began first and the words to fit it came much later.

He should have known as soon as they got to the pond. Hermine could hardly wait to get out there, so he let her go while he took the time to pull on his shoes inside the recreation building where it was warm.

When he finally clomped out to the edge of the ice, his feet already felt frozen solid and attached to foolish rubber ankles. A horde of skaters skimmed the pond like black gulls, effortless in their flight and stronger than tigers. Out of that mob he picked Hermine at once because he had a knack of looking exactly in her direction as if compelled to do so.

She didn't surprise him at all because she danced the same way, light as a floating cattail seed blown into the wind by natural explosion. Seeing her told him something, however. Skating required more than just skates; it needed poise, purpose, and above all strength. Hermine had them all.

He thought she was showing off for his benefit. Sometimes she did that, but not tonight. He saw at once that she belonged here among the scudding kids, young and older, and the salt and pepper sprinkling of adults who still needed to feel that youth was with them one more night.

The pond had ice scrapings turned yellow under the lights and thin music drifted from the recreation building to give the darkness a pulse. He headed toward the edge, feeling the iron ridges of the frozen ground where mud ruts had taken shape to last forever. His ankles buckled with each step and now his legs trembled.

Out on the rim, he saw that Hermine would bear watching; she was no ordinary skater. She skimmed the surface without touching it in her own violet shadow, fast and lively. In full flight, she could stop dead to turn or avoid someone else. She skated backward, cut a figure, warbled a poem of movement that left him oddly ashamed. Then she was talking with a boy she knew, an idiot in a red wool cap which dangled a sweep of decoration, and she abruptly put both her hands in his. Together the couple spun the full circle of the pond and stopped front center.

"Hi," she said, disentangling from the stranger's filthy, loathsome paws. "Lon, this is Terry. He goes to Whitefish Bay and my sister knows him well." She laughed. "He cuts her lawn all summer and my sister wants to know plenty about anyone who does that. He's Irish, he says."

"Hi, Lon," Terry flung across his heavy white sweater, crisscrossed with a band of tartan clan knitting. His teeth flashed white in a reckless smile, the kind to make a girl think of a schooner tacking into the wind and the barefoot captain up in the rigging, acting like Marlon Brando. A guy to hate.

He would be named Terry. A mother gazed at this sleeping, milk-gummed infant and said gently, "We'll name this one Terry." A kid grew to fit the name.

"Hi, Terry," he said automatically while trying hard to at least stand on the ice. His ankles shuddered sickeningly, condensing Butyl rubber from the atmosphere. Sure he could skate, but he'd need another pair of ankles to do it on.

"See you, Hermine," said the incredibly evil Whitefish. "Nice meeting you, Lon. Be around now—"

"Yeah, real nice," Lon said.

Whitefish took off in a terrible clatter of angled running blades, the way a long-legged seabird takes wing by a furious slap of webs across the water.

He shot around the pond in perfect style, cutting his right skate across the left in a fast curve that set him splendidly upright into the straightaway on the other side. Lon had to admit he was good—as good as Ice Follies can get. Too good, maybe.

"Well, come on," Hermine said. She was holding out her mittened hands as if she thought she were Queen Elizabeth on the other side of the puddle. "You might as well begin learning right now, Lon. You know what happened to the California condors. They're almost extinct from not learning how to fly right."

"Where did you hear about condors?" he growled.

"I read about them during my bird days, as Mamma calls them. Didn't I ever tell you about that? Uncle Herman brought me a little parrot from Guatemala, and I fell in love with him. Albert—that was his name."

"Albert?"

"Yes. He was a lovely parrot who could talk and I was awfully fond of him." She tugged on Lon's hands. "Come on. Let's start you on the ice—"

Dutifully he pushed himself outward and teetered there despite her stabilizing grip. She had strong fingers and balanced him with his feet squarely together, as stupid as humanly possible.

He waited in silence.

"You didn't ask," she said in a hurt tone.

112

Lon's arm started to swing in a wide arc, catching his center of gravity and forcing it back into position.

"Ask? Ask what?"

"How anyone twelve years old could be in love with a parrot?"

"Easy," he told her. "You said you were. Everybody likes a parrot."

"True," she admitted, "but very few girls love them tragically. You see, I realized that to love Albert I'd need to be a bird myself, so I practiced for hours. I thought like a bird, talked like one, and—well, everything. I used to fly all the way home from the seventh grade—"

"Ha," he said, "I can see it—"

He began to laugh and the sudden shifting of inner air spun his feet out from under him so that he sat down on the ice that simply. But it wasn't simple; sitting down without the will to sit brought a bone-jarring blow. It was so unexpected that he couldn't let go of her hand fast enough and pulled her right down on top where she twisted around and sat up beside him, shrieking with nutty laughter.

"I've never seen it before," she screamed, meanwhile waving at interested friends from her sitting position. "Every new skater takes some falls, Lon. But they don't do it standing still—" pointing and laughing harder. "Only you, Lon. You're different."

A fall was nothing; he'd fallen a hundred times before without disgrace. But never like this—not pitifully and devoid of honor. Her laughter fell upon brass ears, while a huge rage began small within him and grew like the waste fires in designated areas.

"It isn't funny," he growled in a low tone. "You were

distracting me with all that parrot nonsense, and—well, my legs just scooted out. It could happen to anyone—"

"It wasn't nonsense," Hermine said reproachfully. "Albert was very real—to me. Our love was—"

He saw somebody fall in a majestic, spread-eagled swoop out there on the pond.

"You see—" he hollered, pointing, "anyone can—"

His heart jumped as the supine victim roused himself and took off in a flurry of speed. It was fat Whitefish, the Terry of her choice!

"Hey, how about that?" he yelped. "It was your lover boy—"

She put a finger to her smooth lips.

"My, my," she said thoughtfully. "How wonderfully German you are becoming, Lon! My lover boy! Is this jealousy from Lon Renton? I thought I belonged to you, Tarzan, and you belong to me—or was that a popular song in California?"

"No," he told her, finally locating a weak grin behind clenched teeth. "And don't call me Tarzan. In my country is no good. Kill! Kill!"

"All right. Anyway, I was telling how I used to fly to win Albert's love and then that big science-scare came along. Our teacher—he was big and fat—" She blew out her cheeks to show how fat. "—he taught us about flight. You know, Wilbur and Orville, lift, wing surfaces. He pointed out man's fantastic progress by means of which he can hurtle himself—Well, Lon, surely you know how man hurtles? Ziss, New York! Ziss, Miami Beach! Ziss, San Luis Obispo—"

"Why there?"

"Because you used to live there. At Greyrock." She sighed. "Anyway, I didn't fly home ever again and natu-

114

rally Albert sickened and died of some terrible tropical disease. It was the death of my first love and it nearly finished me with love until you came along, Lon." She gazed at him with a somber, fixed expression. "Lon, the only other thing I ever loved was Albert, until that day at Mitchell Park when you came along. Do you believe that?"

"Yes," he said miserably. "I'd be a cowardly rat to doubt it."

She giggled. "All right. I have your belief. Now do you believe we'd better get up from here right away, because—"

"Why?" he asked, being obstinate. "Why not stay right here and spend the evening? I'm comfortable—"

"That's just it," Hermine told him seriously. "You don't know anything about winter, do you, Lon? You could fall in a snowbank and freeze to death because you were tired. You see, if we sit here we melt the ice a teeny bit, and then— Well, we might not be able to get up in one piece. We might need to be—be engineered out of here in public, and I don't think the kids would forget that sight in a long time—"

Naturally he got right up and she began teaching him. The going was slow and painful, but Hermine was very patient and she didn't even smile anymore when he fell in that helpless attitude and nearly broke his spine.

By the end of the evening he was moving along fairly well alone, taking a tentative try at cutting in a curve, and muffing that, going ahead in the sickening inevitability of motion started tending to remain in motion.

Hermine skated to his side and impulsively held out both her hands to skate with him. "Try," she coaxed. "Just try once."

He did and was astonished at all the strength she carried in her slender body, but of course a big helpless hulk would pull her down. They gave it up.

"—until you're more confident," she explained. "You're doing wonderfully well right now, and in a mon—by the—the end of the season you'll be as good as the—the best—"

She lied to soothe his bruised feelings, of course, and he knew it, but skating had taken too much out of him for argument.

They returned to the recreation building early, despite Hermine's buddies screaming at her not to leave.

Halfway there, Lon knew what was wrong with his skating; he had no control. And why? It wasn't hard to guess. He was frozen all the way to the center, and his feet were entirely gone into numb lumps which were totally separate from the rest of him. How could a person skate with no feet? It wasn't easy.

There was a wood-burning cast-iron stove in the recreation building and in its warm glow, Lon took off his skates and rubbed his disembodied feet with tender solicitude for the white-hot fire first, and then the tingling later. But eventually, life returned to them enough for him to put on his street shoes and go stamping around the room. Ice-skating? That was a true sport.

Later, he found Hermine curled up in one of the big chairs and staring hypnotized at the curls of flame from the stove's interior.

"Have you been waiting too long?" he asked.

She looked up at him with what could only be tender devotion.

"A while," she admitted, "but I sat here and made up stories, about—about us—"

"Like what?"

116

She looked away. "I made believe we were married," she said without a trace of mawkishness. "We live in a white bungalow in California. Roses trail along the fence in splashes of scarlet." She smiled with guileless pleasure. "We have—lots of children and they're all home, scrubbed and waiting for dinner. I'm at the window—the kitchen window with scalloped café curtains. Know what I'm looking for?"

"Orange blossoms," he said. "Nectarines. Gold nuggets between the patio flagstones—"

"Of course," she said simply, ignoring him. "I'm looking for you when you drive up in this small car and you get out, carrying your—"

"Briefcase?"

She shook her head. "Tools," she said, "and you keep out of this. It's my dream—"

"All right—"

She went on. "So you come in the house. You're still awfully young, but you're growing older—"

"Naturally. If I didn't, it would mean—"

"Quit that, Lon," she told him. "And then I—"

"Kiss me—"

"I do nothing of the kind," Hermine said with dignity.

"Why not? I've had a rough day—"

"What if you have? So have I. Doing all that washing, cooking, cleaning, scrubbing, baking, waxing, polishing—"

"Stop!" he cried. "What do you do?"

She took a breath. "I hand you a nice cup of coffee," she said, "and then, if you like, I kiss you—"

There was a silence.

"Say now—" he told her softly.

She stood up. "Let's go, Lon," she said. "I feel so happy. You're nice."

117

He had Thelma's Buick tonight on their theory that a person needed transportation at least part of the time. Behind them the chains slapped their metallic teeth into the ice crust on the pavement, and the ancient heater oozed a trickle of warmth.

Beside him, Hermine was snuggled into a self-contained cocoon, where only her face showed. Once again, he felt that her presence was an allusion to all things of the earth that were lovely and warmly personal—trees, sky, the patina of moonlight.

In this small universe he felt secure and needed, if only for a few minutes. Yet for the first time since coming here, he experienced a definite sense of belonging to a certain region, a special slice of the world. He knew he would never learn to skate this season or any other to compete with those who seemed to have been born on skates. He was of the West tonight, as much as any frontiersman ever was. The Pacific slope was in his blood and thoughts, and he would always be a stranger in this town.

Knowing that, admitting it, somewhere within him the formless plan begun tonight pressed toward his consciousness, demanding some specific shape. Yet Lon wasn't aware of it; he only knew that he'd lost his dark mood and in its place had come an unusual buoyancy. Even Hermine noticed, but she realized as well as anyone that teen-agers had unreliable emotions that rose and fell like the tides.

For no reason, he said, "How much longer is it until Christmas vacation, Hermine?"

She couldn't remember but she was willing to calculate the days if need be, counting them out on her fingers, and his too. Hermine was easily infected by his temper, especially when he was happy.

"Why?" she asked. "Do you really need to know?"

"Not really," he said. "Merely got to wondering how long—"

"Is school so awful that you want to count days?"

"No," truthfully, "it isn't half bad. Boring, naturally, but what isn't? Look—" glancing her way, "it was just a question. Ordinary people ask it all the time—how many days until Christmas?"

He changed the subject, but he was still puzzled why merely asking how long it was in days made him feel exceptionally light and free—as if Christmas vacation was mighty special.

As it turned out, Christmas was important this year. It was the turning point in his whole life.

9

FOR A WHILE after that first evening, Lon couldn't understand why all the old hostility he'd felt at Greyrock returned to him. It couldn't be the weather, although he hated it. Naturally, winter in Milwaukee was bound to be different from that he had known before, and besides, making weather a life problem was childish.

Yet he flunked one of Miss Foelske's major tests, where he had the answers cold and simply blocked them out of his mind for that one hour. Not only this mistake, but he'd given Mr. Lehrer a wise answer to a question that brought a laugh in class and scored him down at the bottom of the heap in the teacher's estimation. It wasn't good.

Silly as it seemed, he had to admit it was important—almost urgent—for him to master ice-skating and get out there with Hermine and all the ease and cool style the other guys had to offer.

From then on he had attacked the ponds like an enemy over which he knew he had a long-term advantage no matter how many victories it scored against him. It was only a skill—a sport. All a person needed was plenty of practice, so he vowed to learn how or die in the attempt, an alternative he very nearly accomplished a couple of times in brutal falls.

He did make progress, enough to know that his failure as a skater had nothing to do with his mood. Sure, it wasn't the kind of improvement he demanded of himself, a miraculous change, but it was noticeable.

His efforts did have the effect of diverting Hermine from her buddies. A couple of times she even left them in mid-circle and skimmed to his side to retrieve what bony wreckage might be saved. Each time he got up and gave her the cheery smile as one who would not be deterred by trivia such as a crushed clavicle, he would ask what she had in mind.

Hermine was honest. "I—I'm afraid you'll hurt yourself —" and realizing too late how damaging to the male ego was such a fear, added, "—accidentally, of course. I don't think you'd do it—"

"On purpose?" he'd finished.

Getting mildly damaged was the understatement of the season, he figured, because on at least one occasion he had been certain he'd fractured an entire backbone.

Nevertheless, he'd forced himself to chuckle, through teeth clenched in anguish. "You ought to know by now that nothing normal can hurt a Greyrock man, Hermine. He can only cloud his precious honor."

It was an actual paraphrase of one of Captain Dart's favorite sayings out there on the drill field, spoken so frequently that a lot of the cadets believed it.

Then Lon sent her back to her skating partner, contending that she was interfering in the practice he needed to become the finest pair of blades in the crazy north. She'd followed orders, looking worried and terribly cute in her muffler and bright outfit.

But in time she'd gone scared.

"I'm tired of skating," she'd said as recently as last night when they were on their way home from Mitchell Park, walking. "It's boring, just going around a silly pond—" She traced a circle in frosty space with a mittened finger. "Let's go tobogganing next time, Lon." She smiled up at him wistfully as if bramblebushes had kept her from that scene until he came along. "It's so much fun, and you said—"

He beat her to that one.

"I've been tobogganing, sure. I told you that."

It meant going to Mammoth or Yosemite snow a couple of times, where he'd tried the slopes for an hour or more in a rented toboggan. Nothing to it; a person was already sitting down for that sport and in the right pair of pants it didn't matter. But here in the home of the deepfreeze it was probably another case of life or death.

"No," he'd told her positively, "this season it's ice-skating or nothing."

"Why?"

"Because I'm going to learn to skate this month," he said. "You've got me out there as the clown of the ice and now I figure on sticking with it."

He did, too. And it was while executing his last real fall that he finally recognized what the trouble was that had been bothering him. He made a decision.

By now he'd at least been able to churn up tremendous speed on skates and that was a compensation, even though he had no control.

On this occasion, he'd really made the high knots along

the outer edges of the pond. Then at maximum he hit a stick frozen into the ice and it sent him sprawling forward at about fifty miles an hour.

Once down there scudding along, he discovered that it was a little bit like body surfing at Avila Beach although considerably cooler. Body surfing had helped him think, too, and so did self-sledding.

When he stood up and dusted off the slush, there was the idea full-blown in his mind where it had been right along. Hermine came cutting up to him.

"Lon," she gasped breathlessly, "are you hurt? Did the—"

He laughed. "Yes to both questions, Hermine," he said.

He stood there, glaring down at her and shaky still in the ankles.

"What are—" she began.

"Look," he said, "let's face it. I'm a lousy skater and my style doesn't seem to change. But I did think of something else that's interesting. Would you mind a lot if I took you home? I want to talk with you about important stuff."

"How important?" she asked, worried. Lately, they'd discussed some truly important subjects a time or two.

"You'll see," he promised.

"All right," she said immediately. "Wait here a minute. I'll go tell—" She shook her head. "No, I won't tell any of them. We'll go right now, Lon."

They left the recreation house at once, but it wasn't until they reached the street that Lon had finally phrased what he meant to tell her.

They had planned to take a bus home tonight because it was bitterly cold, but he preferred being out here with Hermine alone under the icy stars.

"Mind walking?" he asked. "I mean, for a little way at least—"

She blew a cloud of smoky breath that froze a white path across her muffler. "No," she said, "but—"

"I realize it's cold," he told her, stamping his feet around to demonstrate that he had human feelings too. "But I've got an idea to tell you and I don't want anyone else to hear it. We can get a bus down the street a couple of blocks."

She nodded and they set off together walking.

"I'm going to quit school at Christmas vacation," he told her in a careless tone. "Then I'm going to find a job."

Hermine gasped. "No!" she said explosively. "No, you aren't, Lon. I—I just won't let you do it. Why, we're both seniors. We—we wouldn't graduate together."

He let her go on as long as she liked, waiting for her voice to unwind and at the same time noticing how really cold it had become, so that the breath he inhaled felt sharp and somehow hot.

"Why? Why, Lon?" Hermine finished almost in a wail.

He'd planned this so he spoke softly. "So I can marry you, Hermine. What else? I want to do it now, not next year or this summer or at some future time. Now! Just as soon as I'm able to get a job to support us."

She had her arm through his and was walking close, but she stepped away entirely and stopped.

"Marry?" she asked, her eyes wide. "Now?"

He took both her hands. "That's the general idea," he said. "That's exactly the purpose."

As Lon drew her toward him, she came forward almost reluctantly. When she was near enough, he bent and kissed her just as a car full of kids went by, whooping.

"Watch it, Renton," some joker yelled. "We see you."

Lon paid no attention to anything but the answer Hermine gave him with chilly lips. They started walking together again, ignoring the knives of cold.

"Listen for a while," he begged. "Let me tell you what I have on my mind, and then decide. You can say how foolish it is for people our age to quit high school, and how hard it'll be for me to find a decent job. Say that all you like, Hermine, and I won't argue—not if you let me tell you a few of my reasons first."

"All right," she said.

They walked all the way home, and for Lon it might as well have been April, with Milwaukee blanketed by roses blooming in the fields of ice.

As he talked, he was aware of the flimsy foundation of his plan where so much of its success would depend on long-shot luck. He admitted that a diploma was the minimum educational requirement for most jobs. But there were plenty of strong advantages to balance that handicap. In June, for instance, that month so far off in the unfulfilled future, every guy in the city would be out looking for work. But in December there would be practically no competition at all for the permanent jobs. All those coming diplomas would still be in school.

"What kind of job would you want?" Hermine asked.

Lon was practical; he let her know that. "It probably wouldn't be much," he agreed. "Every guy has to start somewhere a long distance down the scale. I'd be—well, almost anything they wanted: a shipping clerk, say, or an apprentice in a trade. Anything to get going. I'd need to hit them all and take what I could find."

"But would you earn—"

He broke in on that. "Enough money? You're going to talk about that? These days a shipping clerk earns a fair salary, Hermine, and I wouldn't be a shipping clerk very long. We'd get enough to live on while I made a start. All we'd need would be a small—apartment, I suppose, and—" He swung full around and faced her, walking backward. "Would you mind? I mean, for a little while—just getting along—"

"Turn around this minute," she commanded, "and walk in the right way, Lon. You'll slip on the sidewalk and—"

"O.K.," he told her. But before he did he kissed her again and found his answer. No, Hermine wasn't going to mind. She loved him no matter how small the apartment or the salary, so he didn't ask her again.

He put his arm lightly across her shoulder and began to talk about that magic land ahead when they would be finally free. He foresaw that funny little apartment up high somewhere in the building with its inconvenient kitchen and its tiny, all-purpose room that had been transformed by the catalyst of love to the most fabulous place in the world.

There they would be lighthearted and brave for the first few months until they found something better. Meanwhile Hermine would make the apartment over with a few cans of paint, her deft skill with art and decoration, and an unbounded, unfettered imagination. There they would both maintain their individuality, and the quarters would be modern and neat, a place to invite good friends.

Before long, Hermine was visualizing the apartment herself and even selecting curtain material that could be pinned and tied without sewing, because Lon knew very well what an awful seamstress she was. She would use

127

low floor cushions of foam, a print or two on the walls, and Japanese shoji screens and paper lampshades to delineate floor space and cast a warm glow everywhere.

"But what would I do all day?" she asked suddenly.

He hadn't given that much thought. "Well—" he began.

"I could get a job, too," abruptly. "Then we wouldn't have to live in such a dingy place, Lon. We could rent a better apartment."

"No," he said severely. "My wife doesn't work."

"Why not?" she asked with genuine curiosity. "My sister—"

It was one of the details which needed a little more planning. "No," he repeated. "No job for you."

"But what would I do?"

He was faintly annoyed by her persistence. "How do I know this early?" he inquired. "You'd probably keep right on going to school because it would only be a semester."

"Lon," she asked in perplexity, "if it's right for you to quit school, why isn't it all right for me?"

"Not the same," he said. "It isn't the same at all."

"I think it is—in a way," she answered, "but—" She didn't say anything more about that subject, apparently accepting differences.

Riding home on the bus after he'd left her, Lon knew he had scored heavily. The Mannheims weren't the sort who insisted on college, and Mr. Mannheim hadn't finished high school himself, although Mrs. Mannheim had done so. But Hermine would recall that her father and mother had married in their teens and had done mighty well.

It didn't take him long to understand why the idea of dropping out of the whole scene had occurred to him tonight. It wasn't a new idea. He'd thought about it the

128

whole time since he'd entered Greyrock, but in a sub-merged way. He'd hated school from that moment on and hated the senseless authority vested in adults who had no visible qualifications for command.

He had to admit that school in Milwaukee had been all right even though he was in the general course which was conducted with heavy, fat books and much emphasis on the academic assignments. Yet this was an industrial city as anyone could see, smell, or hear while the steamers hooted out across Lake Michigan with their cargoes of ore and machine tools. Those sounds could reach a person sitting at a classroom desk.

Also he'd told the truth that jobs for high school kids would be scarcer in June than in January. Maybe a senior with a good story about urgency and economic need would stand a better chance in the competition even without a diploma.

Slowly his plan began to take on concrete substance instead of the fiction he'd spun for Hermine. He had only the vaguest notion about how a teen-ager could actually get married, and indeed, marriage had been little more than another word to him until now. But as he thought it over and saw Hermine and himself in that Japanese apart-ment somewhere in the city, being married to her seemed already a casual fact requiring little further effort. Some red tape, sure. But not much more.

He reached home still spinning his story of the future. Thelma, who was up and reading in the family room, noticed a change.

"Why, Lon," she said, glancing from her book but keep-ing a finger in tidy place, "you look positively glowing with happiness. Did you have a very good time this evening?"

129

"Yes," he said without thinking. He had been happy, at that.

"Your skating is getting better?" Thelma inquired.

"No," he told her. "I'm a rotten skater and I guess I'm never going to catch on. At least not this year."

"Not this year?" she said. "Well, it isn't so surprising, Lon. I had a friend who visited from Florida once, long ago, and she didn't learn at all."

Lon kept silent, feeling neighborly to that Florida chum who had probably caught on right away and scooted back to the oranges and everglades.

"Then it must be something else tonight," Thelma mused.

"Yes," he nodded. "I—I came to a decision. A big one." He concealed the note of triumph in his voice.

"Oh, now I understand. Yes, it always makes a person feel better to think problems through to a decision." She went back to her reading.

At least she was different, Lon decided as he plodded upstairs. Most adults would have wanted to know exactly what sort of decision could be so important to a teen-ager. But Thelma stopped at the boundaries of a person's right to individuality. In that instant of recognition, he thought that it might even be possible to confide in his stepmother and get her opinion about dropping from school. But he didn't dare risk it. He hit the sack and slept dreamlessly.

The next morning began a new life for Lon. He saw the world from a different angle, kept secret now, but soon to be revealed.

His first reaction to school was a disdainful separation from it which lasted a couple of days while he let the work drone by. He'd seen plenty of people do it that way. They sat back for a semester or even a full year in the quiet vacuum of their own intentions. They were silent, usually, creating no trouble and contributing almost nothing.

Yet Lon didn't want to go out like that. He made his peace with Mr. Lehrer and Miss Foelske and took up the work assignments as if he planned to be in this high school forever. He could stand anything for a couple of weeks.

Meanwhile, he spun his story to Hermine, adding the dreams and gingerbread until she was entirely hooked by its spell. Now, she, too, could see life shining ahead—first the small job as shipping clerk while Lon finished high school at continuation or night classes—then the advancement to a better apartment or a house of their own.

They even quarreled over some of the nonexistent details, and made up right afterward. Hermine wanted to move to California at once, but Lon held back. His plan was to start with a good company and stay with the firm a long time.

Not until later would he admit to her that the reason he didn't want to take out for California was because of the lies he'd told that girl about all the sugarplum trees and fancy toys spread around the place. He knew as well as anyone that California was worse by far than Milwaukee, except for the climate. Jobs for teen-agers in that promised land were as scarce as diamonds loose in the streets.

Once, as the time drew near, she asked a funny question.

"Lon," she said, with her eyes troubled, "I know you've made up your mind. But have you told your stepmother and your father? Do they know about us yet?"

He hesitated only an instant. "They know," he said.

"Really, Lon?" she asked, her seriousness deepening.

"Sure," he returned irritably. "Think I'd lie to you?"

131

Hermine searched his eyes for one second and turned away. Then she laughed so that people in the school corridor where they stood turned to look at her.

"What's so funny?" he growled.

"Nothing," she managed.

"Must be something."

She faced him. "I was laughing about your telling a lie. You don't ever lie, but you do get—"

"Get what?"

"Carried away with—" she tried hard to explain without hurting his feelings, "oh, with loving me and wanting to— to be nice, I suppose. It's like all that lovely story you told me about California. Remember?"

"Yeah," he said. Then he told the truth. "I haven't said it to Thelma in so many words, Hermine. But I've admitted that I'd made a decision and that something was up. Is that good enough?"

"No," she replied strongly. "It wouldn't be fair. You can't count on adults understanding you. You have to tell them exactly what in so many words, and you know that, Lon. So—please—you will tell them?"

"I guess," he finally said, feeling uneasy.

10

LON POSTPONED telling Thelma and his father as long as he could, but Hermine kept after him the whole time—which was fairly strange conduct for someone who'd said she couldn't bear her own parents.

"Sure, sure I'll tell them," Lon had protested, "as soon as the right time comes around. They always have something else on their minds."

Hermine accepted that excuse for a while, but not for long. "It sounds to me as if you're scared to tell them," she'd scoffed. "Maybe you don't want to quit school at all, and that's why."

"The real reason I haven't told them," he admitted, "is that I don't know whether I can get a job or not. Shouldn't I wait until I have the job?"

"No," firmly. "You should tell them now—the whole thing."

"About us getting married, and—"

"Why not?" She shot him a challenging glance. "That is, if you still plan to marry me. Or maybe you were just talking."

"Just talking!" he yelled. "You mean, about loving you and—"

She nodded. "Yes, if that's what you were talking about." Her eyes widened with pure innocence. "Why, if you can't tell your stepmother about getting married, how would you expect me to explain to my father?"

He knew at once that she'd won her point and that he might as well start making up with her as to slide into a quarrel. He'd learned by experience that if he owned up to his abysmal stupidity right away, her womanly generosity would permit her to forget. It saved time and was probably all he deserved for being in love with a girl who had tried to be worthy of a parrot.

"I'll tell them tonight," he promised.

As it developed, he wasn't going to need an appropriate moment because one was brought to him.

"Lon," Thelma asked at the dinner table that night, "have you been feeling well lately?"

He glanced up in surprise. "Of course," he said. "Never better."

His stepmother went on about how she'd been noticing an unusual quality in his behavior lately.

"You've seemed so preoccupied," she told him, "and your father and I have been wondering whether you were ill." Thelma smiled. "Or if you were in some kind of trouble we don't understand."

"I'm not sick," he answered directly, knowing that this was the time to tell them. "Maybe it's because I've been doing a lot of thinking the past few days."

"Thinking?" his dad asked, evidently trying to visualize the process in a teen-ager. "About what?"

"School," he said bluntly. "I've been thinking about that."

"School?"

"Yes. I've been wondering whether it's right for me to keep on."

Both his dad and Thelma spoke together. "Right!" they exclaimed. "School?" Almost nobody was against education.

"Yes," he said, warming to the subject. "I mean, should I let you keep me in school when I really don't see any use to it."

There was a silence that developed heavily.

A faint, unbelieving smile came to Thelma. "I'm—I'm not sure I understand you, Lon," she said. "Are you telling us that you intend to drop out of high school in the middle of your senior year?"

"Yes," he told them. "I do intend to. I'm going to drop out as soon as vacation begins. I want to get a job and—well, pull my own weight. School is all right, but it's boring, and—It simply doesn't prepare you for the job."

"The job?" asked his father, seeming to awaken from a dream. "Your job, Lon?" He snorted in derision. "Young man," he continued heavily, "you listen to me. Why do you suppose we got you out here all the way from California?" rhetorically. "It was to allow you to finish high school and if possible to send you on to college. So that is what you will do, do you hear? You will not drop out of school. That's a direct order."

Lon had a rehearsed answer to a direct order; it was a direct countermand. Yet he hesitated to issue it because he didn't want a big battle about his decision. Not yet, anyway.

"Yes, sir," he said. "I heard you."

Thelma began speaking; she knew plenty of statistics about school dropouts. Lon wasn't in the pattern at all.

135

Half the parents of dropouts were in the unskilled labor class with many unemployed. Most dropouts couldn't read above the sixth-grade level and were achieving far below their abilities. Over two thirds of them had never participated in extracurricular activities, especially in large schools, and lack of interest and success were the reasons most frequently given for dropping out by the students themselves.

"It's a tragedy, Lon," Thelma said, "because seven or eight hundred thousand boys and girls drop out each year, and most of them have great trouble finding employment. At least 20 percent of all teen-agers available to the labor force are unemployed, and the dropout has the least chance of any of them."

"But—" Lon began, "that doesn't mean—"

"I'm sorry, dear," Thelma said, reading the dark message in his drawn brows and smoldering eyes. "I've been talking as if you are a statistical case, when you're a very special person with your own reasons. Perhaps you'd like to tell your father and me—"

For the first time Lon could remember, his father broke in to interrupt Thelma.

"I'd rather the boy didn't," Harold Renton said curtly. "Not here at the dinner table." He spoke directly to Lon. "Young man, not even the services want boys who haven't finished high school." That was that, evidently. He put down his napkin and rose to his feet, staring down disdainfully.

Thelma's voice was almost protective. "Lon's not exactly a boy, Harold. He's more mature than most. I shouldn't be surprised that you did find employment, Lon, but it would be such a waste."

His dad snorted. "A waste. Not while he talks nonsense.

I'll hear no more about it. Please excuse me." He stalked
from the table into the family room, trailing silence.

For a while, Lon seethed with resentment. He'd been
right about telling them. He should have waited until he
had the job. But no, Hermine thought she knew better.

"I shouldn't have brought this up," he told his stepmother.

"I'm glad you told us," Thelma replied, trying to sound
reassuring, "and I practically forced you to. Let's set it
aside awhile, think it over, and perhaps when you've made
up your mind to discuss it again, why—"

He could picture that time about a hundred years from
now. "All right," he said.

Thelma stood to clear the table and Lon helped. Then
he went upstairs to his room without telephoning Hermine
as he usually did on the few evenings he was home.

As he sat alone, his resolve to drop school mounted to a
passion. He wanted to leave at once, to get out of their
house and never come back to bother them again.

But gradually some practical sense crept in. He had no
money and no place to go, and their reaction had really
been unexpectedly mild. It could have resulted in an
enormous scene, with people yelling about how ungrateful
and stupid he was.

Nobody had come upstairs to give him a little private
talk, and gradually he relaxed. At least he'd kept his
promise to Hermine.

At the breakfast table in the morning nothing was said
about the night before. Both Thelma and his father were
busy people with precise schedules of work to be done.
They maintained a false cheerfulness the whole time, and
a little later, left the house. That was that.

Their apathy gave him a sense of impending victory.

137

Like most adults, they possessed neither the energy nor time to talk it over with him. He needed only to keep quiet, find a job, and spring it on them and they would probably shrug and tell him there was nothing they could do.

That morning, Hermine could tell what had happened. She seemed able to read his mind or something.

"You talked with your father and stepmother!" she said.

"Yes," he came back, "I said I would, didn't I?"

"How did they take it, Lon?"

He snapped his fingers. "Like that. Nothing to it."

"Like that?" she mimicked. "I don't think I believe you."

"Why not?"

"Because they aren't like that. Not Miss—not your stepmother. Tell me what they did say, Lon."

He shrugged. "They didn't like it," he replied, "but I know that everything's going to be all right in a few days. You wait and see."

That was how the thing stood right up until the close of school for the holidays. Lon didn't waste any time at all. On the first Monday of vacation, he left the house early and hit the pavement, going first to four employment agencies that were willing to accept his application. One even had a vacancy in the stock control of a retail store, but as the personnel man was writing out the card, the company phoned to say that the position had been filled.

He got around to a couple of other places on his own, and at one of them, the Behrman Company, which manufactured furniture, a Mr. Lennox took his application and asked him questions, seeming to be interested.

The day was gone when he headed toward home and because it was so late he went directly to Hermine's. She opened the door when he rang the bell, but instead of asking him inside she stepped out on the porch and whispered that she had something she wanted to tell him. She was already wearing her coat and things as if she'd been waiting there for him to arrive.

They walked a while in silence.

"What's up?" he asked, worried. "Why the mystery?"

"Nothing," she said.

He grinned. "Why don't you ask me where I've been all day?"

"I don't need to," she said. "You've been out looking for a job."

"How do you know?"

"Lon," said Hermine, eyes narrowing and sounding exasperated, "anyone can tell where you've been. You've got ink on your fingers, and besides—"

"Besides?" he inquired. "Besides what?"

She tossed her head disdainfully. "Why don't you ask me where I've been today?" she demanded.

"Hey!" he said. "It is a mystery. All right, where have you been today, Sherlock?"

"It isn't mysterious," Hermine insisted. "It's—it's—"

"What?"

"Maddening," she said. "I'm mad. Can't you tell?"

He searched her face for the usual signs. When Hermine was only a little bit mad, she could laugh. But if she had genuine rage, she cried. He didn't recognize symptoms.

"Where have you been today?" he repeated.

"At your house. That's where!"

He made an exclamation. "My house! Why?"

"Because I was invited. That's usually the reason, isn't it?"

He didn't need to muddle his brains around, or play dumb either.

"Thelma?" he asked.

She smiled. "Yes. My old kindergarten teacher of by-gone years. She telephoned and asked if I could call on her at a certain time. Naturally, I could. And did."

"But why?"

"You guess." She glared at him. "Go ahead. Take a chance."

He turned to her sharply. "Let's quit playing any games about this, Hermine," he said. "It's probably too serious. What did that old—what did Thelma want?"

She didn't answer. "You know, Lon," she said, "there's an awful lot of gracious glassware in your house. My, my! Pretty."

"Stop that," he implored. "Tell me what it was."

Hermine drew herself up to her full five feet two. "Nothing, really," she said, twiddling her fingers out-stretched. "We had tea together up there in your cold house. She served it in those little painted teacups, Havi-land, I think." Hermine put her hands on her hips and took a couple of mincing steps down the sidewalk. "La-de-da!" she said airily. "It was a special blend, imported from"—glancing up at Lon—"one of those good places in Asia."

He took a long breath. "Hermine," he said severely, "cut it out. Tell me what you talked about, so we can—"

"Tea," she said, turning away from him. "The merits of tea. The weather; school affairs; trends in fashion. Little things like that which go with tea—" She came back to him, squinting her eyes. "Lon, your stepmother could never be German. Potter. Miss Thelma Potter. That must be English. Yes, especially with tea."

140

"Hermine," he implored, "please! Tell me what went on. Tell what Thelma said about us."

She grew very cool. "You don't believe me, do you?" she said. "You never really believed me, did you?"

He caught her hands tightly. "Cut that out, will you?" he almost yelled at her. "So you had tea. Big deal. You talked about the weather, clothes. I'm supposed to believe that?"

"Yes," she said. Suddenly she broke into that wild kind of laughter he'd heard the first day when they'd met and ridden along the shore. Then she subsided quickly and put her arm in his with sudden warmth. "I'm sorry, Lon," she told him. "I suppose I've been a little frightened about spending a social afternoon with your stepmother. Actually she's terribly nice, when a person gets—gets accustomed to her ways. It was good hot tea. Hot—" She giggled. "You'd need plenty of hot tea in your house, Lon. It's so c-cold!"

"There wasn't anything else?"

She hesitated. "Nothing, really. I guess she just wanted to find out what kind of girl I am—"

Lon's voice was dark. "What kind of girl!" he exploded. "She doesn't have the right to ask you that. She knows what kind—"

"Yes she does," Hermine answered quickly. "She certainly does have the right, Lon. Uh—let's go back. It's getting dark—"

They headed toward home and the mood changed. He told her about the employment agencies, the silly questions, the long forms. "Mr. Lennox, out at Behrman's, seemed encouraging," he finished. "Oh, and I even gave your father's name as a recommendation. Do you think he'll give me a good reference?"

Hermine giggled, and made a face. "Oh, yes. Papa will say that you ought to go far."

"It isn't a joke," he said dourly. "I'm going to hit the factories every day from here on out. I'll get a job or die in the attempt!"

"Just like you ice-skate?" Hermine asked.

"Not exactly," he said, grinning with some rue, "but with the same general idea—"

"Then I'm sure you'll find a job, Lon," she said seriously, "quit school, do anything you want—"

"And marry you?" he teased gently.

She nodded and her eyes were very soft.

"I guess so," she said. "But shouldn't you finish school? I mean, wouldn't it be better for everybody if you had your high school diploma? And then—Well, your brothers went through college, and—"

"Who told you that?" he asked. "About my brothers?"

Her eyes hid themselves behind lashes. "You did, Lon. You've talked about them many times."

"I suppose I have, but—"

He saw the house ahead and spoke rapidly while he had the chance. He said that life wasn't all a matter of the usual rules; there had to be exceptions.

"I love you, Hermine," he finished. "It's as simple and as complicated as that. Do you believe me? How about that? You're always asking whether I believe you or not."

"Yes," said his lovely girl, "I do believe you, Lon. And that's the trouble."

142

11

FINALLY CHRISTMAS came and what Thelma had told Lon when he first arrived in Milwaukee was true, but a person had to see for himself to understand the unbelievable. She really did put a candle in every window of the house, and kept them all burning until after midnight.

Lon went outside to see what it looked like from the street, and there in all the windows the flame burned and cast waves of red gold upon the frosty windows.

He noticed a man standing beside him there in the yard.

"It's fantastic," the man said. "I didn't believe her at first. Did you?"

Lon started. "Dad," he said. "It's you." Then, "No, I didn't think—"

"Nobody would unless they saw it," the older man agreed. "Try to imagine running up and down those flights of stairs to watch more than a hundred candles, any one of which could set fire to the house. Yet she's been doing that insane thing for over twenty-five years."

"I know," Lon said.

143

They returned to the house together and sat in the living room where the Christmas tree stood. For the first time since that barren day at Greyrock, Lon felt a warmth toward his father—a sort of understanding.

Once or twice they both lifted their eyes toward the ceiling as faint footsteps passed overhead and doors opened and closed. Thelma had told them she needed no help. She'd kept all those candles burning so many times before that she had developed a routine that was easier if she worked alone.

Lon was suddenly aware of how difficult life could have become for his father who had to fit a routine as fixed as that candle-lighting ceremony. Tonight he looked unusually old and tired, as if he endured a special kind of loneliness.

"I tried to tell her she'd burn the house down doing this," Mr. Renton said as if to himself, "but she won't change it a bit. You'd think candles down here on the first floor would be enough. But no, she's had them in every window clear to the attic and she intends to keep it that way." He shrugged and chuckled to himself.

"It's awfully pretty," Lon said, "I mean, from the outside. People even stop their cars to look."

"I know. I saw them. You have idiots in every part of the country."

There was a long silence between them while the lights on the tree winked on and off, and Thelma came downstairs like a wraith, passing silently through the room.

Lon noticed that she was flushed from running up and down the stairs, and once again he had the feeling that the house was inhabited more by ghosts than living people. He was sorry that he had refused Hermine's invitation to spend Christmas Eve at her house.

"I ought to be up there with Thelma and my father," he'd explained, and she'd understood.

Hermine was talking more and more lately about how foolish it would be for him to leave school now, and he was beginning to agree. He'd been everywhere and most places had turned him down so flat he'd begun to give up hope. Thelma had been right about the unemployment statistics for teen-agers, except that hers were too low.

Lon almost brought up the subject with his dad, recalling that unpleasant scene at the dinner table and wanting to say he was sorry it had happened. As long as no jobs were available, there wasn't much use to talk about it at all, though. Even one of the personnel men had discussed staying in school long enough to get a diploma, which had disturbed Lon enough so that he'd almost told the man he hadn't come here for advice; what he needed was a job. All the adults felt the same way, evidently.

So he didn't say anything to his father. Besides, the wind had come up outside and was moaning down the chimneys and rattling the storm windows that weren't frozen solid. Aware of that, Mr. Renton got to his feet, muttering, and went upstairs. Lon could hear him up there arguing, and probably saying that with a wind like that draught in the fireplace, some candles ought to be put out before they set fire to the curtains. But it didn't do any good. He came back a few minutes later and dropped heavily into a chair.

"Christmas!" he announced to nobody in particular, but Lon understood what he meant. The candles—all of them—were going to stay lighted even though a tornado struck. It was Thelma's tradition and she meant to abide by it no matter what.

Mr. Renton switched on the radio and listened to Christmas carols, and Lon read the sports section in the news-

145

paper. It was so much like Christmas at Greyrock that it was funny, and sick—the way the hours dragged into midnight.

That was the moment of snuffing, with an order for putting out the candles exactly the opposite of how they were lighted. Thelma had a silver candle snuffer that she used, starting in the tower first and dropping the dead candle into her apron, pinned up to make a sort of bag. When all was done she came into the room looking radiant from exertion.

"All finished," she cried, "and a Merry Christmas!"

They opened the few presents under the tree. Thelma had bought Lon clothing—a nice sweater, T-shirts, some socks. He'd remembered to give them each something— a necktie for his dad and a scarf for Thelma which she pretended to have been craving all year.

It was dismal, and a hard lump came into Lon's throat and stuck there the whole time although he stayed with the ceremony until Thelma served them cake and cocoa and Christmas was over.

He was about to turn away gratefully and go upstairs to bed when the phone rang. It was Hermine, wishing him a Merry Christmas and reminding him that she truly loved him, she knew not why.

"Don't forget to be here tomorrow. Come early," she said.

The Mannheims made a big thing of Christmas, the time when there were thirty different flavors of cookies. They opened gifts in the early morning, as Hermine had described, and there would be one under the tree for him. She used an old German phrase to tell him of it which she finally said meant "A silver nothing and a gold wait-awhile." Something like that. Her father had teased her every year since she was a little girl with the same words.

"I'll be there," he told her.

He was embarrassed already by the gift he'd found for her. It was a tiny Swiss watch in a crown ring setting, imported and inexpensive, but fairly neat looking. Hermine didn't need a watch; if anyone cared not at all for the time of day it was that girl. But it had caught his eye in one of the downtown stores and he'd bought it, regretting his impulse almost immediately.

"How is Hermine?" Thelma inquired after he hung up.

"Fine," he told her, wondering again about that afternoon when she'd asked Hermine to the house. A dozen times he'd almost opened the subject to learn what had gone on, but he didn't.

"She's such a darling girl, Lon," Thelma said. "I'm so glad you like each other."

"Thanks," he replied. Then he excused himself and went upstairs.

Christmas Day was big enough. The Mannheims had showered all their children with gifts that Mrs. Mannheim had been storing up the whole year, from skates and toys for the grandchildren to household items for Hilda and Eva.

Lon found himself sitting in on a big, rousing Christmas celebration. He wore his gift from Hermine which was also a wristwatch, but a sturdy American make with a reputation for accuracy.

Hermine had run around with her gift as if it were one of the old crown jewels of the Austrian empire, but the more she showed it the more ridiculous it looked to Lon, and he wished he'd bought her something else.

147

They spent part of the afternoon chasing the kids around with their toys and then going by themselves to see what Marie Gottlieb and some of Hermine's other friends had received for Christmas. Afterward, they went to a movie.

When he left Hermine at her door, she kissed him lightly. "Thanks for the gift," she said, "it's the nicest one I ever got, Lon, and I love you. Do you believe that?"

He didn't answer directly. Instead, "I can't remember a Christmas like this one. It was—well, kind of wonderful."

"Do you?" she begged, her arms still around him.

"Do I what?"

"Believe me."

He looked away from her, down the snow-blanketed street where the corner lamps struck off golden pools of light.

"I've believed you ever since that first day at the park," he said in a low voice. "Every day, more and more. I can't think of anything else except how I believe you and how much I hope that—" He let it go there.

"I know," she said, her voice brightening. "And it'll all come true. But don't you think we shouldn't try rushing things? We're both awfully young, and—"

"Young?" he asked, nettled. "Who's been talking to you? That's what they all say—about how young we are. I can't help being young—"

She stepped back. "I didn't mean it that way. It's only that—Oh, Lon, every Christmas I feel like such a kid, and I get sort of scared."

"Scared?"

"Yes. About growing up. At Christmas the world seems so big, and—and frightening. Do you know what I mean?"

He knew, all right. He'd felt that way his whole life, he

148

guessed—that the world was big and frightening, waiting out there to gobble a person down. So he cringed back and clung to childhood with all his strength.

"No," he said, telling the lie, "I don't know what you mean. Look, Hermine, I know Christmas is a big day at home for you, with all your family. But it's different with me. I've got to get out of childhood and grow up, and nobody told me how young to be when I did it, or how old. All I know about is the time—" He glanced at the new watch winking gold at his wrist. "I can see it down here—" pointing, "—and the time is now for me."

Silence.

She shivered. "I'm cold," she said. "We'd better go inside."

He stayed a while with her, talking about the day and a dozen other details that had nothing to do with his problem. After that he went home and Christmas was over for Lon Renton, ending as usual on a note of failure, with Thelma's candles as good a symbol as any.

Thelma had been right: there weren't any jobs for someone like him, so he could either roam the streets or get back in school. "Where you belong," they would tell him, whether they knew anything about him or the school.

Nevertheless, Lon kept at it in the week before the New Year, going out early and making the rounds, and becoming more discouraged every day. Some of them said, "I wish you'd been here last week. We had a place in the shipping department for a young fellow with your determination."

Kind words; they had plenty of those to give away, but little more.

149

He used a practiced approach, making himself sound eager, yet with exactly the right humility in his tone. As he gained experience in their questions, he created ready answers. Quite a few wanted to know why he was leaving school, and to those he said that the problem was economic. He couldn't go on expecting his poor parents to support him forever; they wanted him to continue school, but it was plain they didn't have the money. It was his idea, he said, to work and get his diploma in night classes, the way many a successful man had done.

But finally that Monday morning rolled around and it was time to return to classes. When he met Hermine that morning, she was terribly eager to get to school, something unusual for her.

"What's the rush?" he asked. "Can't remember you so anxious about the books."

"It's not that," she said.

"Then what?"

"I had an idea about us," she told him. "I mean, for this next semester."

He thought that over. It wasn't in Hermine's nature to have school ideas that involved them both with the future, so he took this one cagily.

"All right," he said, "let me guess. You've thought up something to get us both interested more in school. You don't want me to quit and locate that job so I can find the apartment—"

"No—" she snapped, but then changed her mind. "Well, you did guess it. But what's wrong with wanting to keep you in school? You haven't found a job yet, and—" She trailed off.

Lon thought it over coolly. There wasn't anything wrong—except that it reminded him of what a stupe he'd been, spinning the story and reaching an anticlimax like this. "Nothing wrong," he told her. "Nothing, except that it makes me feel worse for not getting a job as you say."

"Oh, Lon," she cried impulsively, linking her arm through his in that same possessive manner, "you shouldn't say that. I didn't mean to hurt your feelings. Why, everyone is interested; you've said so yourself."

"Not interested enough," he said dismally.

"But—" thinking fast, "you expect things to happen just that quick—" snapping her mittened fingers soundlessly. "Why—why even Hilda's husband Jerry had trouble finding work last fall, and he's—He's in the union and everything. One of the best men in his craft. So—"

Lon wanted to change the subject and avoid the quarrel brewing. "Sure," he said. "So all right. What's your big idea about school?"

"Oh, that—" with false enthusiasm. "Why, I thought we could both get into some extracurricular activity in our last semester. We could—well, work on the school newspaper—uh, you know, be reporters or something. Or there's the senior play. We could try out for parts, and—"

"Join the Art Club?" he asked lazily. She hadn't been to a meeting of that great group in months.

"Say—that's an idea. I'm already in that, you know," Hermine said.

"Yeah. I do know."

"Why didn't I think of that before? You could join the Art Club, and—"

He couldn't help himself; he laughed.

"Hermine," he said as soon as he realized it wasn't funny, "you're cute; too cute. Somewhere you learned that if people are in activities they don't drop school. So now you want me in the senior play, is that it?"

Her lips grew round as she framed the denial, but then she shrugged. "You got me," she sighed. "Officer, I'll never do it again, so help me. How did you ever catch me?"

"Easy," he told her loftily, "fingerprints. As every schoolboy knows, there are no two fingerprints alike. Also, I can read your thoughts—"

"Oh, no you can't," she declared. "Because if you did, do you know what would happen?"

"I'd sign up for play tryouts?"

"No. You'd be dropping dead right in that snowbank." She laughed. "Only don't do it. I need you, Lon. For what, I don't know."

By the time they'd reached school, Lon had decided not to give up so easily, and that afternoon he let Hermine walk home alone, or with whatever buddies she chose. For himself, he caught a bus downtown and made it to the Acme Employment Agency just before closing time.

"No, nothing now, Renton," said the tall man—a Mr. Miller, "but keep checking back with—"

He seemed to remember something, and fumbled with papers on his desk. "Renton. Lon Renton," he mused. "Yes, here it is. On Thursday, Mr. Renton, we did have a position for you. Last Thursday we called this number. It was a very good company, too. An office boy was what we needed—"

"You c-called Thursday?" Lon stuttered.

"Yes. I have the note here. Your mother answered and said—let me see—" reading a scrawl, "yes, here it is. 'Says he is already employed.' I knew I'd seen your name in this inactive basket. We put your application on inactive. Do you want to reactivate your papers?"

"She said I'd already been employed," he answered through anger. And then more smoothly, "That was my stepmother. I—I had a couple days of temporary work during vacation and I suppose that was what she meant." He faced Miller with unwavering eyes. "It was one of those misunderstandings, I'm sure. Yes, I do wish you'd reactivate my file. And I'll check back." He turned. "The job—I suppose it was filled?"

"Oh, yes," said Mr. Miller. "We have a lot of applications, you know, and this was a real opportunity for a young fellow with the right attitude. But we'll keep you in mind. Call back."

Out on the street, Lon found the other agencies closed so he rode home choked with a black rage. He hadn't failed to get a job. One had even chased him, until Thelma, that—that woman had lied. She preferred letting a guy think he was a total failure.

When he reached the house he went in through the back door and up the stairs, although Thelma heard him and called, "Is that you, Lon?"

He didn't answer. Instead he went directly to his room and dug out his old suitcase from under the bed, opening it and staring within where his clothes would soon be packed.

From a corner of the top drawer of the chest he brought out the last of his money, counting it twice and adding that to what he had in his pockets. The total came to less than four dollars, and that wasn't enough. He couldn't even rent a room for a couple of nights, probably, let alone eat.

He knew what he had to do. He couldn't leave tonight without money, so he went across the hall, filled the washbowl, and dipped his face in cold water, drying carefully

153

and combing his hair, and thus bringing his calculated anger under control. Slowly he smoothed his features to fit the picture of a carefree teen-ager home from another great day.

It was a good trick, and when he remembered it in later times, it was always with shame. His whole attitude, from that bleak summer with his brother, through Greyrock and the first half of this year had been nothing but a training in subterfuge and illusion designed for a boy in hiding.

When Thelma called him, he went downstairs to dinner, despising his stepmother for her acts and his father for setting the stage. Yet the whole time he was speciously relaxed, courteous, and even pleasant in his tone—as if this were a role in the senior play.

"You seem happier tonight," Thelma said with a smile. "Did you have a good day?"

"It was fine," he replied with an appalling innocence. "Hermine wants us to get into a few extracurricular activities next semester. Like the senior play. She wants us to try out for that."

Thelma nearly blushed, which was strange. "Hermine— She wants you to do that?"

"Yes," he babbled on, "and I think it's a good idea, don't you, Dad?"

Mr. Renton came to life. "Oh, by all means," he said. "Activities would be fine. Do you think your schoolwork is good enough?"

"Of course it is," Thelma cut in jubilantly. "My, my! The senior play! Lon, would you believe that I had the lead in our senior play? And—Of course the schools were ever so much smaller then—why, there were hardly enough

154

boys in the class to fill the roles, and now there is all that competition in a huge school. But I do wish you luck. Hermine is so pretty; she's likely to be chosen at once. And as for you, I'm certain you could play any part you chose. You may not know it, Lon, but you're quite talented."

He met her eyes unflinchingly so that it was her glance that turned away first. "Thanks," he said modestly, "but I don't think I have much talent at all."

"But you do," Thelma said.

With dinner over, he waited an appropriate interval and even offered to dry the dishes.

"No, I'll take care of everything tonight," Thelma said in a preoccupied manner. "You probably have a date— you still call them 'dates,' don't you?"

He did. A standing one. When he left, Thelma almost forced him to take her car, but tonight he stuck with an iron refusal.

"No," he told them. "The pavements are too slick and I have a hunch I could wind up with trouble. Thanks a lot, but I'll take the bus, the same as always."

It was a tense evening, and more than once Hermine demanded to know what was the matter, thinking herself responsible.

"It was stupid of me to suggest getting into activities," she said, trying to smooth everything over. "But I thought it might help us, although I knew you wouldn't want to."

"Forget it," he told her gruffly. "I keep telling you it isn't that. I'm just—well, moody tonight—"

"Tell me," she wheedled.

He wanted to in the worst way, but he knew that he even had to distrust Hermine. If he told her his plans, she'd hit the telephone as soon as he was around the corner. In that respect, she was like the adults. Hermine thought she knew better than he did about how to act in life.

"There's nothing to tell," he insisted. "Don't you ever feel a little bit anxious, as if you had something in your mind that wouldn't go away, and yet you didn't know what it was or what to do about it?"

"Yes," she said. "But not often. You've made me feel that way sometimes—as if I had to do something about you, only I didn't know what that was, or how."

"Hey, thanks for the compliment," he grinned.

In a while they were both laughing about his ornery nature, obstinacy, and plain foolishness.

He left her in a good mood, with his own plans secret. And as he lay sleepless toward dawn, it came to him that a guy couldn't trust anyone with the things he meant to do; the ones he had to do if he went on living with himself.

12

B^{Y THE NEXT} morning, he had it all figured. He waited alone in the empty house until the telephone rang as he knew it would. Hermine was calling from the pay station at high school, her voice trembling with anxiety.

"I'm sorry to have worried you," he said, "but it was too late for me to call you at home when it happened. I'm sick with this upset—No, I don't think I'll be in school today."

He described the malady and the details of how it had grabbed him, but only after she demanded to know. Yes, he was going to the doctor. With that she seemed satisfied.

"I'll call you at noon," she told him.

"Don't do that."

"Why not?"

"I won't be here," he said, putting a little truth into the conversation. "I'll either be in Dr. Schmid's office, or I'll be headed back to school."

Finally, Hermine was willing to wait until he called her at home late this afternoon.

When she hung up, he returned to what he'd been doing at the little desk in the front sitting room. He sat huddled there in his overcoat, moving the pen with scrupulous care.

The note was short. It told both Thelma and his father what he had done—left home—and that he knew about the job offer she'd turned down for him, but that it didn't matter. There would be other jobs.

He thanked them for their help in bringing him to Milwaukee and making a place for him in their home. But he said that they would all be better off if he went his own way, now that he was old enough to decide for himself. He signed it simply, "Lon," and put the sheet of paper on the dining room table, where it couldn't be missed.

His packed suitcase was ready and he'd made a neat bundle of the other things, so important to his plans. He made a quick and final inspection of the room. The chest and closet were empty. His first intention was to leave everything they'd bought him, but it was a childish gesture to hurt somebody's feelings, and besides, he couldn't have left without the stuff.

The bed was made and he'd swept the room, putting everything of no value in the trash receptacle down in the basement. A last look around was enough; he left the place without glancing back because if he had any regrets he didn't know what they were.

The suitcase was heavy and he was glad to set it down at the bus stop on the corner. When a bus came along he got in and paid his fare, noting with satisfaction that there were plenty of seats. When he passed Mannheim's Market, he didn't even look outside.

158

He dismounted at the edge of the downtown area where he remembered a couple of places he wanted to go. The first was a loan company where he laid out the belongings that might be worth money.

Everything he had—a transistor radio, skates, his overcoat, and a small camera brought only ten dollars.

Lon was astonished, and said so.

The owner shrugged. "Take it or leave it, sonny," he said in a way that meant he couldn't care less.

Lon took the tickets and the bill, holding them in his hand for a moment of decision. Suddenly he stripped off the watch Hermine had given him.

"How about this?" he asked.

The proprietor looked it over carefully. "Nice watch," he commented, "new. You sure you want to part with it?"

Lon didn't reply.

"For the watch I can give another ten dollars," the man said. "But no more. This is a business here; we've got to make a profit."

Wordlessly, Lon took back the watch and slipped it over his wrist. He reached for the door.

"You've got thirty days on these other items," the man said. "We hold them that long before we sell. Come in and get them back."

Lon nodded and got out of there.

He was lucky about finding a room only a block from there, the sort of place where the clerk wouldn't ask questions about being so young. Lon reached it up a flight of dark stairs that had a brutal stench at the bottom of the well that eased off nearer the top.

A large room at the landing had ratty old chairs covered with cracked leatherette. The desk at one side had a bell which he rang. The man who appeared had been sleeping heavily, or so his red-rimmed eyes indicated. Yes, he had a vacant room for two dollars a night.

"How much a week?" Lon asked.

"Eight bucks," the clerk said, rubbing his stubbled chin with a big-knuckled hand. A tattoo showed on his forearm, an anchor piercing a heart with some initials above and below that design.

As Lon fished out his wallet, he noticed the clerk's eyes watching, counting the money, too. He found the ten and got his change.

The clerk yawned. "You from around here?" he inquired.

Lon had his story ready. "Not exactly," he said. "I'm really from California: San Luis Obispo. But I've been out here since September visiting my stepmother. I'm looking for a job and I figured it would be easier on us all if I lived down here while I looked."

The clerk blinked and accepted the story, perhaps because it was so near the truth that it would be too much work to prove it a lie.

He found a key attached to a piece of red plastic, embossed with the number "37."

"Room's upstairs," he said, pointing to the staircase at the far end of the lobby. "Turn left at the floor and go down the hall. Bathroom is down farther a few doors. You'll find it."

Lon took the key, aware that the clerk's eyes still followed him with an insolent scrutiny, but without question. Another man had come up the stairs behind Lon, an individual needing a shave and a clean shirt as much as a room. He came to the desk while Lon moved toward the staircase, aware that the clerk's attention had shifted to the newcomer.

The carpeting on these stairs was a florid, intricate design much stained and worn. The hallway at the landing went both directions, so Lon turned left and found the number he sought.

The room was narrow and dank, with a window opening into a ventilation well which appeared to be impenetrable to the sun. There was a stained washbowl, a closet of puny proportions, a small table, and of course the bed, all of them clean to a man's standards—with no regard for corners or unseen places.

He set down his suitcase and tried the lock on the door to find out if it would work from the inside. Surprisingly, it did, so he pushed the bolt and sank down on the bed.

At once he was aware of a grisly, sawing noise. He listened intently and with some apprehension until he realized it was a man's fulsome snore and that the incredible sound came up the well. Beyond that, there was nothing except the city outside, screeching and hooting down the distances where incessant wheels made a scuffing background to everything else.

The same odor he'd noticed in the well at the street was here too, but covered by another that had a piney chemical impact. Unaware that he did, Lon recognized the smell. It was that of lonely men—hundreds of them —who had sat here in this room through years and years of despair.

Lon didn't stay here long. There was an oppressive sensation that grew stronger by the minute until human snores were a welcome, ordinary sound. The room, he discovered, had a voice of its own, a gentle rustling that seemed within the walls, and a movement that the floor adopted every few minutes.

He stood abruptly and turned on the light which at twenty-five watts of naked bulb served only to intensify the gloom. In the uncertain illumination, he counted his remaining money and calculated how much time he had. Not over a week, if he ate only one hamburger twice a day. Also, he'd need bus fare to get around.

Such monetary urgency drove him into the hallway. The bathroom wasn't as dirty as some, nor much cleaner than others. There was a roller towel attached to the wall, recently used, but he was able to turn it to its last clean surface. Then he left.

It was only noon. He stopped at a small stand and bought one hamburger and a glass of milk which he hardly enjoyed, so appalled was he by the check, fifty-five cents. He couldn't go on eating this well for very long, he told himself.

Because employment agencies were quiescent during the noon hour, on impulse he decided to take one last shot at the furniture factory—the Behrman Company.

He remembered Mr. Lennox, a tight-mouthed young man who wore glasses and who had seemed interested in Lon's reasons for going to work.

"Keep coming back," Lennox had said. "We may have something for you later on."

It was a long bus ride, but Lon reached the three-story factory building and went directly to the personnel office on the first floor.

The same young brunet was there. She asked him to sit down. Then she rapped on the inner office door and went inside.

A moment later, Mr. Lennox emerged and spotted Lon,

motioning him to come inside while the brunet went to the filing cases to locate papers which she brought back with her and put on the desk.

"Sit down—" Mr. Lennox said almost cordially. He glanced through the papers. "Lon Renton, is it? H'mm!"

Then he began to talk. He said that making plenty of calls was one of the most important things a young person hunting a job could do, and that Lon already seemed to understand it.

A couple of hours later, he was outside the building again. Mr. Lennox, it seemed, had gone to work when he was sixteen under almost exactly the same conditions. To his knowledge, the experience and lack of education at the moment hadn't hurt Mr. Lennox a particle. Although Lon was young, he'd decided to take a chance and place him in a junior timekeeper's job in the trim-cutting department.

That turned out to be a section of the factory devoted to power sewing machines operated by women and a few men at the cutting tables. Automation certainly hadn't taken over here quite yet.

The long bolts of upholstery fabric were spread out on a huge table, marked to pattern, and were cut with power equipment. These pieces lay around the sewing room in metal carts to be deftly sewed together by the women who worked by the hour. They earned a bonus for piecework, which was entered on time slips. It was the timekeeper's duty to keep track of the slips.

The senior timekeeper, a man named Kepler, explained the work to Lon, and Mr. Lennox told him to report on the job at eight the following morning.

That quickly, everything opened up for him—so fast he felt dazed. But he came out of that in a hurry; he had

163

plenty to do this afternoon. He hurried back to the hotel, took a shower, and headed for Hermine's. He wanted to catch her before she got home and called Thelma.

Lon barely made it, but today life had begun to work out. He'd just gotten off the bus in front of her father's store when he saw her coming down the sidewalk from school. He dashed across the street and met her on the opposite corner.

"What are you doing here?" she wanted to know. "You're—why, Lon, you're supposed to be sick—"

"I'm not, though," he said.

He began telling her how Thelma had kept him from getting a job and how he'd left this morning, checked in at the hotel, and gone out at once. Then plain luck had come his way; he'd found the job, a good one with a decent starting wage. The whole plan had suddenly clicked into place, and—

"Hey!" he said suddenly, "look at you!"

"M-me?" Hermine gasped. "Why me?"

"Didn't you hear?" he demanded. "Didn't you get what I said? I've found a job. I can leave school and earn some money—"

She was silent.

"And how do you take it?" he asked. "How do you react? Why as if you'd heard bad news. You look as if you wanted to cry, that's what—instead of being glad, and—"

"Let's walk around the block," she said in a low voice. "I can see my father over there in the market. He's going to look out of the window and wonder what his crazy daughter is doing today."

They moved slowly down the sidewalk. No, Lon thought, he wasn't ever going to understand Hermine, but that didn't matter. How could anyone understand a girl who was as lovely as a bunch of wild flowers?

"Lon—"finally, "do you remember the day—well, that tea party I had with Thelma. The one I started to tell you about?"

"Yes. How could I forget it? Does it have—"

"A lot," she finished. "It has a lot to do with us, Lon, because it wasn't really a tea party at all. I—I suppose I fibbed to you because I had a kind of fight with your step-mother and I didn't tell you. You see, I—well, I told her to mind her own business and that I could very well look after mine."

He thought that over. "Good," he said, "but I still don't get it."

"Of course you don't," Hermine sighed. "Nobody who wasn't there could understand. You were gone—out job-hunting, I think—when she telephoned. She asked me to visit, so of course I went. We sat in that ice-cold little sitting room of yours—"

"It's not mine," Lon interrupted. "If it were mine, I'd—"

Hermine shook her head. "It's more yours than you think," she told him in an odd voice which carried plenty of significance. "You know that Miss Potter—I mean, Thelma—used to be my teacher? I didn't tell anyone I was going there because she seemed awfully disturbed—"

"How could you tell?"

"I could, that's all."

"What did she want that was so important?"

Hermine glanced at him hard. "That's how I felt when I went there; I wondered what that—that old—teacher could want of me. Lon, I found out that she wanted me to help her; she said—"

"Help her? With what?"

Hermine held out her hands in that gesture of hers, fingers spread wide. "You," she replied. "She wanted me to help her with you."

There was a silence.

Then, "You're kidding me."

"No, I am not," she said seriously. "As soon as I was in the door, Thelma said, 'Hermine, you're probably wondering why I asked you here. It's because I'm beside myself with a problem and I think you may be able to help me with it.' Those were her words, Lon. Not exactly, but near enough. I got the same feeling you have—that she was going to put me down, as you say. I got angry right away—"

Her upturned eyes were filled with the recollection.

"Why shouldn't you be mad?" he demanded protectively. "What right did Thelma have to abuse you, merely because—"

"No, no, Lon," she cried. "Don't say it that way because if anyone got abused it was your stepmother. I was terrible to her; I—I didn't treat her nicely at all—the same way I've sometimes been to my own parents."

She seemed to be asking him for understanding.

"Oh, I get it," he said.

"I don't think you do," Hermine told him. "You couldn't. She brought in the tea service and put it on a small table —all those delicately painted cups and the teapot there with those little silver spoons she has that are so terribly old. And the cream and sugar in—Why—" Hermine's lips trembled. "I naturally thought she was trying to—to snub me. We sat opposite each other in that chilly room —the one with the—the black marble fireplace, and here was the tea. I thought she was trying to shame me—to put

166

me in my—my place. So I gave it right back to her, you know—in an exaggerated way, really mocking her. It was awful—"

Lon didn't know what to say, so he laughed. "Forget it," he told her. "Tea—what was she trying to do to you?"

"I was angry," Hermine went on softly, as if she hadn't heard him. "I couldn't think. Lon, if it had been anyone else but Miss Potter I would have cried. There she sat, so tall and—and stern. I was always kind of afraid of her when I was a little girl, and I suppose I still—"

"What did she say?"

"A lot of things I didn't understand then, but I do now. She said that she was a teacher, and being a teacher is different from being a mother. Mostly, she talked about you, Lon—"

"Me?"

"I was going to tell you all about it that day, remember. But I didn't, because I changed my mind. She talked about being a spinster, she said, for all those years, and marrying someone who was a widower with grown sons. She talked about being a stepmother—how it was, and so on—"

"You tell me what she said about us!"

Hermine went on in a flat tone. "She said she realized her limitations in 'reaching you' as she called it, especially when you are 'so withdrawn.' She's tried very hard to talk with you about dropping out of school, but she knows how futile that is. So—"

Hermine's voice choked with emotion, and tears suddenly bloomed. "Lon," she finally managed, "she said, 'I asked you here because I know you can help me, Hermine. Lon is terribly fond of you—perhaps he loves you, although it's difficult for older people to understand

167

how love can be so real with someone so young.' I didn't understand what Thelma was doing then. But I do now, and it's haunted me ever since. Do you know why, Lon?"

"No," he said truthfully. "I sure don't." Nuts, probably.

"It was her remark about being young. I got mad there," Hermine said. "I told her that she shouldn't interfere in your decisions, and that I couldn't convince you any more than she, and if you wanted to leave school perhaps it was because you were still young enough to make up your mind."

"That's right," he said. "Let's forget Thelma and all of them. I want you to promise me you'll marry me as soon as I—"

She broke in. "But don't you see what Thelma was really saying, Lon? She wasn't trying to put me down at all with her silly tea party. She was telling me that we're equals because we have something in common that no other two women in the whole world possess."

Now he did laugh. "You—" he gasped. "You have something in common with my stepmother? Man, that tops everything. What is it?"

Hermine faced him. "Lon," she said, looking up with an expression he would remember—almost pleading. "Thelma was telling me that she loved you too. She wanted to help you. She was saying that she lost you somewhere because she doesn't speak our language. She was begging me to help her, because she knew I loved you as much—as much—"

Meeting Hermine's eyes, Lon had a stupid thought of that watch he wore. "Ten dollars," the man had said, and he'd very nearly taken it. Maybe life was like that: a series of snap decisions; the breaks.

168

Now here was this sentimental slush about his stepmother, imposed upon the reality of today, of Mr. Lennox who was willing to take a chance on a guy he didn't know. And those women with the power sewing machines: they were in a tough, true world.

"Look," he said in a hard, new voice, "forget that. Later on we can talk about it, if you still want to. What I need to know is when you'll marry me. In a couple of weeks, I'll have money, and we can—"

"I don't know, Lon," Hermine said in a faraway voice, "except that it can't be until you get your diploma. I won't marry you now, not even if my parents would let me."

"Wh—" he began, as if she had hit him a blow.

He stood there, trying to comprehend. This was impossible and yet he'd heard her say it.

"But why?" he said, his voice rising. "Why?" his voice dropping lower. Reasoning, "It was—Why just three weeks ago we—we were arguing about how to decorate the apartment. I just don't understand you, Hermine."

"I don't either," she said. "But I do know that I love you, Lon. Don't you see? Oh, please try to. Thelma's right. You're a person who has to finish school—high school— maybe college. You'd—why you'd die if you didn't. And if someone loves you, she'd be willing to wait as long— As long as she has to."

"I still don't get it," he repeated, shaking his head. "You love me so much you won't marry me, although last month—" He performed an elaborate gesture, like throwing off heavy weights. "It's a mighty strange style of showing a person love, I guess. And my wonderful stepmother, Thelma, made you see it?"

"Yes," Hermine Mannheim said with simple dignity.

"She taught me something about love. I was a long time learning."

His anger came slowly because Hermine was beautiful —a silver kitten, a golden bird, her dark hair cut wild, glossy, to frame her oval face made delicate by a wide, full-lipped mouth; someone charged with warm lightning who belonged to him. This girl—

Still he felt cheated and tricked. They began to quarrel, and he dug the knife deeper and deeper. Finally, he took her to her door.

"Good-by, Hermine," he said in a wooden tone. "I'll phone you."

She whispered to him. "Please, Lon—" begging. "Don't go away. Wait—wait until we're not mad anymore. Gives us both a little time to think it over, and—"

"Good-by," he said again.

He turned and strode away from the most wonderful girl in the world. Afterward he couldn't guess why he'd been so arrogant, proud, and cruel.

Sure, he phoned her that night and for a minute or so it seemed that all was right again. She sounded so glad.

"Aren't you coming home—I mean, here to see me? Tonight?"

He nearly gave in, because the truth was he'd ached with regret every moment since he'd left her.

"Well-l—" he began.

Then, "Lon," innocently, "you may not like this, but I telephoned Thel— I phoned your stepmother and told her about—"

"You didn't!" he sputtered.

"Yes," she said in a childish voice. "I—I had to, Lon. Don't you see?"

170

His tone was low and cold. "You had to!" he mocked. "Why?"

"I just did, Lon," she said tremulously. "It—well, it merely happened. I did, just the way I'm having to tell you now, and—"

"Don't bother," he snarled and banged down the receiver.

It was only then that he remembered he hadn't told her the name of this hotel, but only mentioned the district it was in. Well, he was glad of that.

He went upstairs and hit the sack, trying hard to sleep. Instead, he lay wide awake in the narrow room while the walls rustled their unseen message of mildew and hopelessness, and far away the wheels of traffic grumbled ceaselessly.

13

LON KNEW at last that this was right where he'd come in—at the destination toward which that Greyhound bus from the west had always headed.

He'd lived through a week of this misery, a full seven days of a black void wherein he had not heard one single syllable of Hermine's light voice. Instead, he'd learned the meaning of pride—that dark tower of the human spirit which was so easy to mount and so nearly impossible to descend.

The walls of his dirty little hotel room had closed around him each grimy night, and there he'd endured his pain alone.

By day he did what he had to do—pushed on the smile and went the rounds of the trim-cutting department at Behrman's. He caught on quickly enough, as both Mr. Kepler and Mr. Lennox said. He was fast at sorting and tabulating the work slips, and accurate in the furious posting at the end of each day. But nothing from either Kepler or Lennox could have cured Lon of his sickness, because he was sick with pride and remorse and self-doubts.

The timekeeper's office was a cubbyhole near the cutting tables from which Lon passed into the huge room where the women worked. In this vast place the smell of fabric dust was always present despite air conditioning. There the women bent over their machines and with flying fingers worked in a kind of fury and unconcern that was outrageous enough to be a nightmare.

There, Lon had begun to notice already a Mrs. R. Papke, the name she wrote on her time slips, and he didn't know why.

Mrs. Papke was distinguished in the timekeeper's office because she was high every day, far ahead of the others in the number of pieces she sewed together. Discovering that almost at once, Lon began to study her without realizing that he did, as if Mrs. Papke had meaning for him as yet undisclosed.

"What's the 'R' for?" he'd asked Kepler. "I mean, here on Mrs. Papke's tickets?"

Kepler was short and plump. At the top of his head was a growing bald spot over which he combed his fine blond hair. But by the end of the day, the hair had strayed and the bald spot stood out to reflect light from the powerful fluorescent fixtures overhead.

He chuckled. "Rose," he said. "Her name's Rose. That's how we make out her checks. Some rose, hah, Renton?"

"Yeah," Lon laughed. But within himself he wasn't at all surprised. Her name seemed to suit somehow.

At first Lon supposed that it had become a habit of his to watch Mrs. Papke at work because he wanted to find out what sort of woman made the best operator.

There was nothing about her appearance to indicate she had that sort of speed. She was a short, wiry woman, and might even be called frail except that the muscles of her forearm stood out as she moved the fabric rapidly through the stitch with her face close to the working parts of the machine. She wore glasses behind which her small dark eyes beaded, and she tied her hair at the neck so that it stretched down flat on her head and across her ears. She held her mouth tight, and across her upper lip a faint suggestion of darkness grew, yet she might have been pretty long ago.

Schulz, the other timekeeper, called her Champ. "How did Champ do today?" he'd ask whoever was posting her slips. Then he'd laugh. "She's a machine. How would you like to go home to that kind of an old lady, Kepler?"

Kepler would grin. "No, thanks," he'd say. "I'll keep the one I've got—although Mrs. Papke could toss in her paycheck."

After the first week, Lon had thought of moving closer to the factory and had bought copies of the newspaper to look for ads about boardinghouses near that section of town. But he did nothing about moving, and even welcomed the long ride in morning darkness because it helped pass the time.

By now he knew the clerk's name because a sort of shifty familiarity had grown between them. Corcoran had been a seaman most of his life, deep water and lake, as he said. But he'd settled down at last.

"Here at home," he'd told Lon with a smirk, "in Zimmerman's Hotel same as you, Renton," winking horribly so that the red rims of his eyes showed.

He was a small, tough man, scarred by plenty of unclassified battles where he'd lost more often than he'd won, probably.

175

Lon had cashed his first check; though it was small consolation for loneliness it was more money than he'd hoped for. He'd gone to the desk to pay his rent in advance and Corky gave him change.

"Kid," he said as an afterthought, "had a phone call for you today."

Lon took that information like a slap.

"Who was it?"

Corcoran leered. "Some chick," he said in the hoarse whisper he had for a voice. "She asked if somebody named Lon Renton was registered here. I made her tell who she was before I gave an answer. I've got the name written down somewhere. Yeh, here it is: Hermine Mannheim. Know her, or you hiding out from this particular chick?"

"I know her," Lon said.

Corcoran grew serious. "Thought you would. Had a sweet voice. Real sweet. Reminded me of—well, forget that. You better call this chick, Renton."

"Maybe I will," Lon told him and went upstairs.

Sitting alone on his bed, he felt both a surge of gladness that she'd cared enough to find him, and a resurgence to sharp pain of what had become only a dull ache. It was as if a nerve had been suddenly exposed.

He held off minute by minute, but at last he could stand himself no longer. He went down to the lobby and dialed the number, certain of what would happen. They would quarrel, naturally. It would have been better if she hadn't found him.

Mrs. Mannheim answered.

"Lon," she cried out as soon as she'd heard his voice, which embarrassed him. But Hermine was there at once.

"Oh, Lon," she chattered, "I'm so glad. Lon, I've been calling everywhere, every night. Why—why did you have to go away?"

He tried to tell her why—that it really wasn't a choice, but rather, something he had to do for himself no matter what. But she wouldn't listen.

"I know all that," she wailed, "but Lon, you simply have to call your stepmother. You haven't the—well, I know you don't want to worry people this way."

So there it was: the message. He could have guessed it without dropping a dime in any slot. He'd worried them, but nobody ever mentioned how they could worry you.

His voice was cold. "What have I done to poor, poor Thelma?" he asked. "I mean, what now?"

She was reproachful. "Done? Why, Lon—nothing except that you left us all without saying where you were going or where you'd be. That isn't a nice—that isn't the way to treat people who—"

"Who do what?"

"Who love you!" she sort of shrieked.

"All right," he said. "Have you changed your mind about us? I mean about getting married?"

There was a silence that could be measured.

Then, "Can't you come out here and talk with me?" she asked. "I—I can't answer that question over the telephone. You've got to—"

"Got to what?" he said impatiently. "Hermine, you're certainly telling me my business. What do I have to do now?"

"Oh—" she began. "Oh, nothing, you—you—" Her voice half broke and he got the image of her there, half angry, half sad, her brows knit with worry—a girl. "Noth-

177

ing," she said. "Not if you don't know already wh-what to do."

Of course he had to come in with the customary words. "O.K.," drawling it out. "That's what it'll be. Nothing. I'll do absolutely nothing. And what did Thelma say that got you so excited this time?"

"Just that there wasn't a thing we could do but w-wait," Hermine told him, "and she's right."

"Naturally," he said stiffly. "Well, if that's all you wanted, Hermine, we might as well forget it. Good-by."

By real force, he took the receiver away from his ear, holding it long enough to hear a tiny voice in the distance saying, "No. Wait, Lon, please—"

Then he hung up.

He stuck around the lobby a long time, staring out upon the city and waiting for the telephone to ring again. Desperately, he wanted her to call back; yearned for her to try once more. But the phone was mute.

A couple of the old men had come down to sit in the stained chairs, so at last Lon returned to his room with his hands clenched into fists and his mouth full of dry cotton. Time whispered by with its infinite patience.

But Hermine didn't call.

At last he had lived to Saturday afternoon. And one moment he was on the street alone, and the next he glanced up and saw Jerzy Starkiewicz materialize from around a corner. Lon wanted to run, but the guy was already there.

"Hello, Renton," Starky said, showing his bad teeth.

"Starky!" Lon exclaimed. "What are you doing down here?"

He expected the guy to say that this was a free country

and he'd lived all these years believing that an individual could be on any street the law allowed.

Not this time. "I came here looking for you. Hermine told me the name of your hotel, Renton."

"She sent you!"

"No," Starky said contemptuously. "If she had, I wouldn't have come. No, I came on my own, Renton. I don't have time to get sent on errands."

"What's up?"

Starky grinned. "Renton," he said softly, "I made the mistake of thinking you were a friend of mine—the best. I came down here to tell you what a complete fool a friend of mine can make of himself if he gets in and tries real hard."

"That's why?"

"Yeah. That's why."

Strangely, Lon felt no anger. It was something in the manner that Starky had spoken which took out all emotion—as if he was a person who knew what it was to be a fool.

"Maybe," Lon admitted. "You could be right."

"Could be?" Starky said. "Man, I know I'm right."

Together, they went to the corner for hamburgers. Over them, Starky spelled it out in full: that according to his book, anyone at all was an idiot to quit school before they threw him out, and that made Lon the genuine idiotic two-headed baboon boy of all time.

According to Starky, this was an age when every kid needed as much education as he could get to match the kind of world he'd been handed by the wiser heads. He had a sort of gutteral eloquence that reached Lon. His round eyes glittered as he talked, and his crooked thin-

179

lipped mouth held each word just long enough to be diamond clear.

"I came personally to find out if you'd lost your brains somewhere. Anyway, I need you back in that school with me. You gave me some balance—" He paused. "Did you know you're the only person I ever really told about my family? You seemed to understand. And you quit, leaving a girl like Hermine that any of us would give an arm or a hand to know. Renton, you shake me up. I wonder if I should stay, or get out there and be an iron worker where I belong. You shake up everybody, know that? You've got an obligation to come back, Renton. Please—"

But when he was finished, Lon shook his head. "No, I can't," he told Starky. "I don't have a way to go back. I've gone too far already. I guess if I could, I'd take your advice. But I can't."

"Make a way," Starky said fiercely. "Crawl back if you have to. Do anything but this."

"No," said Lon Renton. "I made up my mind."

Thereafter, days merged with weeks at this moment of decision in Lon's life—as if all his future was decided with one spin of the wheel.

He called Hermine again and they quarreled again, but in that time he didn't see her. In the second week he moved out near the plant and he instructed Corcoran to tell nobody his new address.

The clerk shrugged. "Have it your own way, kid," he said, "as long as it's legal. Take it easy."

And that was that, figured down to the last detail.

What he hadn't planned on was Mrs. Rose Papke. She had begun to recognize him and to smile faintly when he went past her machine. So Lon got into the habit of

180

saying, "Good morning, Mrs. Papke," which was as common a thing to do as it could be.

On Monday of the fourth week, Mrs. Papke was absent from work for the day, but returned on Tuesday. Lon noticed at once that there was some different quality to her, but it didn't show until she handed in her time slip. Her production had fallen nearly to the bottom, with deductions for rejects.

Kepler had the answer. "She got new glasses," he said, grinning. "Bifocals. They make her nervous, she says." He swung around on his spring swivel chair. "She's supporting five kids at home, all in school. The oldest is about your age, Renton. In his first year at Marquette. Papke's sun rises and sets in that kid."

That was all. By the end of the week, Mrs. Papke was back on top, never stopping the seams endlessly slipping through her bent fingers. When Lon passed, she'd glance up at him with that same half smile, only now Lon knew what she saw. Mrs. Papke saw her son who was just his age, out there at Marquette and bent over the books.

When Saturday came, Lon Renton went home again, knowing that it meant exactly what Starky had said—crawling back.

He wasn't even a good failure because he hadn't cut every road behind him. Lennox was sore when he told him that he couldn't be a timekeeper for Behrman's any longer. But when Lon left he shook his hand and wished him luck. A strange, quizzical light lay in the man's eyes behind his glasses.

"What are you going to do?" he asked with sincere curiosity.

"I'm not sure," Lon said. "I think I'm going to try to get back in school."

"Think you can?" asked Mr. Lennox.

"No," Lon said. "But I'm going to try."

The personnel man shrugged. "I've heard a lot of young fellows say that. Then they hang around on the streets getting into trouble. Maybe that's what they wanted to find all the time—a chance to hang around doing nothing—"

"Maybe," Lon agreed. "Some people can't fit anywhere. It could be that I—"

Mr. Lennox wouldn't let him finish. "I don't think so," he said. "Renton, it's harder to quit a job you don't belong in than it is to find one—believe me, I know. Most people fit themselves to the job, or try to—" He looked away, out of the window and perhaps along the way of his own life. "I hope you do get back in school. Try to anyway, and if you can't, come back here. Perhaps Behrman's can give you a second chance at being a timekeeper. I'll put your closing check in the mail."

He had taken a while to think the story over, but it hit Lon finally that Mr. Lennox was a decent guy who had been trying to tell him something. With that revelation, a tide spilled over within him that had long been dammed. Truth, maybe.

He'd fought the adult world for years, telling himself that their main stock-in-trade was lies and he still didn't know whether or not he'd been right about that. In one sense, the job in trim-cutting was a lie because it was better done by machines than by human beings, better by far than to have Mrs. Rose Papke sewing her life away to keep a big lunk of a son in college.

182

But people? He had to admit to himself at last that he'd been wrong about them, at least partly. In their own way and time, he knew now that they had all been trying to help him—to be decent, the way Mr. Lennox had been. That old stupe on the bus—Haley, was it? He'd been sincere, actually. It could be that they all felt a sort of obligation to interpret the world for the young; to do their bounden duty, maybe, and in the only way they knew how.

Lon had to swallow hard when he thought of the name, but it was entirely possible that Captain Dart had spoken of his mother in a callous way only because he believed it was the proper technique to snap a guy out of self-pity and homesickness.

He packed his suitcase and got on the bus, intending to carry it up the walk to Thelma's house like a document of total surrender. Sure, he knew what they'd probably say—to get out; that he'd made his choice and he should stick with it.

But a guy did what he had to do, and all Thelma had asked for was understanding, without even trying to explain that the quality was always a two-way street.

He had to go back and tell her in a clear voice that she'd been right—that she, Hermine, and Starky had tried against odds to make him see just one or two sensible ideas.

The bus went past Mannheim's Market and for some nutty reason it reminded him again of Mrs. Rose Papke. He didn't know it then, but someday that woman was destined to be a symbol for Lon of all workers everywhere; those with the hard hands, tough fingers, and strained faces, tired out, unlovely, and strange who toiled without

183

question toward a single goal. It was the Mrs. Papkes of this world, he was sure to learn, who had built the school and begged their young to stay with it and go on to become someone better than the machine, those able to master it and make the gears work for them instead of the job going the other way around.

The bus let him out at the corner and he lugged the heavy suitcase along until he was on the walkway to Thelma's house—a museum, a place for traditions at Christmas, and ghosts.

He glanced at the second story, remembering the hallway with all those doors, and it came to him that a guy could pick any one and pull it open. Although each would be different, he could walk into a room. But the doors had to be unlocked.

Lies? Why, he'd lived one himself, steeped in resentment, with the bolt fastened from the inside and the shades drawn. By instinct he knew what he was doing now—headed inside there to unlock the door, to lift the blinds, to let a little light fall within.

He saw the old Buick in the garage, but his father's car was gone. At the door, he hesitated, wondering whether he should ring the bell.

Lon did push the button and heard the buzzer far off. But nobody came to answer, so he tried the latch. He found it open, and leaving his suitcase in the vestibule, he went within.

Strange! There was nobody at home.

"Thelma!" he called. The name stuck in his throat, so he tried again. "Thelma, are you home?"

He waited, thinking he heard voices muffled and far away.

184

"Lon—" someone cried.

He glanced toward the sound. It was Thelma at the entrance to the dining room. She came forward with long strides, not smiling, but without anger.

"I'm so glad you're home," she said, taking both his hands in hers. "Your father and I have missed you."

"Thelma," he began, using the introduction to the speech he'd worked out, "I've—"

That was as far as he got.

"Lon," she said, leading him forward, "come into the living room where we can talk better. I'm so sorry your father isn't here to see you come home. We've been lonesome here without our boy. My"—turning to him—"you look thin. Have you been getting enough sleep and eating properly?"

"I—"

"But of course you haven't—in a boardinghouse, wasn't it?"

They sat on the settee together and in memory of how truly young he was, Lon gave the speech.

It was about how foolish and proud and brave he'd been to decide to come crawling back, licked by life, a failure nobody could ever forgive—all that old hokum spoken by a million teen-agers before him, no doubt, to get people off their backs. In short, nothing at all.

"I want a second chance," he declared in a lugubrious style. "I know I've lost the first semester, but maybe I can make it up in summer school, and—"

He noticed Thelma looking at him in this peculiar manner—like a kindergarten teacher he'd known long ago. Someone who loved him and who thought that the advice to brush his teeth every day and be a good boy might well take a son all the way to manhood if he had the guts to follow it.

"I've already talked with Mr. Halverman, your principal," Thelma said with a sort of professional compassion.

"Halverman?" Lon asked, wondering what punishment they'd created. The iron cage, maybe, dangled over the edge of the high school as an example to freshmen. "He—"

He told me that if you could return to classes reasonably soon you could go on with your regular schedule and make up the incompletes. You'd need to see your teachers who all speak well of you, Lon, especially Miss Foelske and Mr. Lehrer—"

"Mr. Lehrer? He said—"

My, yes. Mr. Halverman told me that it can be done that way for any sick high school student, so why not— He says many boys drop out because of emotional stress or for several reasons that are unusual. You transferred an excellent record and you've done well on the tests." She looked at him sharply. "Do you really want to go back Lon? You know, your father and I decided that quite possibly we'd been wrong in trying to deter you. Perhaps you needed to make your own decisions, and still do.

"I want to go back," he said, swallowing hard. "Monday."

Suddenly, Thelma smiled in a jaunty, wide manner he'd never seen before.

"How wonderful," she said. "I'm so glad, Lon. I've watched so many of my—I call them my children—" apologetically. "They're so little when they come to me and yet they do grow up and graduate. Why, I haven't missed a high school graduation in thirty years because one or two of them always remember and send me an invitation."

She glanced away, out of the window where memories crowded the yard, shouting there. "But this year—" she said, "this year—"

There was a silence.

"It will be very special," Thelma said, "and—"

Right there the doorbell cut into her thought, loud and so demanding that Lon felt it break some kind of spell. But his stepmother didn't move.

"It must be—" She smiled. "I'm almost sure it is— Oh, you won't like this, Lon. I'm a meddlesome old woman, I suppose, first telling that employment agency that you were already employed at your school, and now this. You see, I noticed you getting off the bus and—"

The bell rang again, shrill, exactly like—

"I telephoned right away. That's probably Hermine, so you'd better answer the door yourself."

It did sound like Hermine. When that girl wanted something she could keep her finger on the button until it stabbed the air, and—

He didn't actually run because there were too many corners to get around, but he reached the front door in record time. Sure enough, it was Hermine. She came into his arms as easily as if she'd been there the whole time.

When he let her go she stepped back and kind of viewed him. "Lon," she announced, "you're so impossibly German that—"

"That what?"

He was watching her closely because she had begun to stamp around the vestibule in exactly the same way she said her father did.

He stood it for an instant, but then he couldn't help himself. Lon blew out his cheeks and began to stamp around with her, in cadence. "You will do this," he bellowed pompously. "You will do that!"

Hermine stopped abruptly and looked him up and down, from head to toe.

"Lon—" she said and there was music in her voice, "all right, I will." She stood on tiptoes to kiss. "I love you," Hermine said.

"You mean after I crawled home this way?" he asked, still protecting his dignity. "What's good about that?"

"A lot," she whispered, making some *ich, bist, dich* sounds, but this time he understood their meaning. A silver nothing, and a gold wait-a-while.

In a moment they went inside. Sure enough, Thelma, the kindergarten teacher, had brewed a pot of tea. She had the little decorated cups and the tiny spoons all laid out exactly as Hermine had described them.

For a while, he watched his stepmother and his girl drink tea together, and like equals exchange ideas—the weather, clothes, trends at school. They called it small talk, he remembered, and it was a good name.

Yes, a guy could open the door and try to accept the world, to understand it. But he knew that there were a couple of things—women and tea, for instance—that he probably would never understand. They had a special message, he guessed. Dumb, but worth listening to now and then.

Biography of James L. Summers

James L. Summers was born in Oshkosh, Wisconsin. When he was a child, his family traveled a great deal, so that he went to school in Wisconsin, Indiana, Illinois, England, Germany, Connecticut, Cuba, Hawaii, Oregon, and finally Arizona, where he graduated from elementary school. After graduating from high school in Milwaukee, Wisconsin, he spent a year in footloose travel in Canada and the United States, and went to sea from Brooklyn as an engine wiper. He visited the West Indies and other ports and finally returned to school at Chaffey Junior College in California. After a year there he matriculated at the University of Wisconsin, but his college days were cut short by illness.

The following year he attended summer session at the University of Southern California, where he met the girl who was to become his wife. They were married the next winter, while Mr. Summers was a student at the University of California at Los Angeles. During the depression Mr. Summers had to leave school, and he worked at many jobs; he was a vacuum-cleaner salesman, a neon-light

189

repairman, a truck driver, and eventually owner of a small electrical business.

Still wanting to finish college, Mr. Summers got a night job, and after two years received his A.B. degree at U.C.L.A. He then started teaching. Writing interested him also, but it was a few years before he sold any stories to the national magazines. One day an editor sold a story for him to *Seventeen* magazine, and from then on he wrote almost exclusively for young people. Now Mr. Summers is writing novels for teen-agers and young adults. His story *Girl Trouble* was selected as an Honor Book by the *New York Herald Tribune*'s Spring Book Festival Committee. *Prom Trouble, Gift Horse, The Karting Crowd, Tiger Terwilliger,* and *The Amazing Mr. Tenterhook* were Junior Literary Guild selections, and *Ring Around Her Finger* was a selection of the Young People's Division of the Literary Guild. Mr. Summers lives in Atascadero, California, and has retired from teaching to make writing a full-time career.